In a Teapot

Books by Terence Faherty:

The Scott Elliott Series
Kill Me Again (1996)
Come Back Dead (1997)
Raise the Devil (2000)

The Owen Keane Series
Deadstick (1991)
Live to Regret (1992)
The Lost Keats (1993)
Die Dreaming (1994)
Prove the Nameless (1996)
The Ordained (1997)
Orion Rising (1999)

Short Fiction
The Confessions of Owen Keane (2005)
In a Teapot: A Scott Elliott Mystery (2005)

In a Teapot

A Scott Elliott Mystery

Terence Faherty

CRUM CREEK PRESS
The Mystery Company
Carmel, Indiana

M
F14

IN A TEAPOT

ISBN: 1-932325-04-2

Cover art by Tim Faherty
Art by Robin Agnew
Book design by Patricia Prather

First published by The Mystery Company, an imprint of Crum Creek Press

First edition: September 2005

Crum Creek Press / The Mystery Company
484 East Carmel Drive #378
Carmel, IN 46032

www.droodreview.com

To the memory of Richard Matthews

ONE

"So there's no killing at all in it? That's a pity."

The bloodthirsty speaker was Patrick J. Maguire, president of the Hollywood Security Agency. "And here's another," he added, tearing a little paper ticket into fourths and tossing the pieces onto the dusty breeze.

As we watched the stragglers finish the race, I slipped my own ticket into my shirt pocket. I'd picked the winning horse for once, but I didn't intend to crow about it. If I got Paddy's competitive blood up, we'd be there till the last race or my last dollar.

"There" was the Santa Anita Racetrack in Arcadia, race-course of the stars. We had a box to ourselves on that hot afternoon, which had given us a choice of places to hang our suit coats. But it had still left Paddy with the considerable challenge of squeezing into the one-size-fits-all chair provided.

In 1948, the year in question, that was quite the squeeze. It had left a good deal of Paddy unprovided for, specifically the barrel chest and the stomach that supported it, a protrusion decorated today with a green and yellow tie as broad as a lobster bib and so loud it made the jockey's silks look like evening attire. His suit was a relatively sedate linen number and his straw fedora had a fashionably broad brim, but his round-lensed sunglasses were strictly prewar, the kind Constance Bennett and her crowd had made popular. This pair looked so tiny on Paddy's broad, moist face that they might actually have been on loan from Miss Bennett's collection.

He turned the cheaters toward me and returned to the conversational line that had been interrupted by the end of the race. "I thought Shakespeare killed them left and right."

"In the tragedies and the histories," I replied. "Not in the comedies and the romances. *The Tempest* is a romance."

"Right," Paddy said, fanning himself with his racing form. "I remember now. All the same, you'd better run through the plot for me. Wouldn't want to make a slip in front of Mr. Jeffries."

Mr. Jeffries was a prospective client of our security firm, the one Paddy owned and I worked for. Why we were meeting Jeffries at a racetrack hadn't been explained to me. I thought we'd gotten there early so Paddy could fill me in, which wasn't my thinking at its best.

"*The Tempest* might be Shakespeare's last play. People like to think it is. It's basically a revenge story. A guy named Prospero, a deposed duke, is living on an island with his daughter Miranda and a sort of ape man named Caliban. Miranda's a beauty. Think Olivia de Haviland, circa 1936."

"Thanks," Paddy said. "Don't mind if I do."

"Prospero is a magician. He has a sprite—a sort of genie—under long-term contract. The sprite, name of Ariel, causes Prospero's old enemies to be shipwrecked on the island, the brother who deposed him and the king who helped him do it. Prospero runs them through a kind of magical obstacle course until they see the error of their ways. Then he forgives them. Curtain."

"There must be more to it than that. Tom and Jerry cartoons have more plot."

"The king's brother, who's also in the party, tries to murder him and Caliban tries to murder Prospero."

"That's better. But where's the romance in this romance?"

"Oh, yeah. The king's son is along for the ride, one Ferdinand. He and Miranda get together, naturally."

"Naturally," Paddy said. "Funny that the love interest should slip your mind, Scotty. And you a guy with one foot on the altar."

It was all I could do to keep from looking at my watch to confirm that a solid forty-eight hours separated me from that particular altar. "While we're on the subject," I said, "this job—whatever it is—can't run much more than a day."

"I'd never dream of interfering with your honeymoon," Paddy replied, passing on the chance to fill in the current blanks.

Of which there were many. All I knew so far was what Paddy had told me the day before: The job had something to do with a recently announced independent production of *The Tempest.*

A lot of independent productions got announced in postwar Hollywood. A few even resulted in movies. But this *Tempest* idea had a gimmick that was already helping it in the free press department. It was being touted as the last bow of the old British Colony.

There was no shortage of British colonies around the world, but Hollywood's little enclave was perhaps the strangest. And the highest paid. It dated from the earliest days of the talkies, when panicked producers had imported actors trained in the legitimate theater by the carload. The British imports had banded together, naturally enough, forming a cricket club, hosting teas, and generally fattening during the lean thirties.

The forties had started the same way. Hollywood had boomed during the war years and the first months of the peace. But now the Paramount ruling had stripped the studios of their theater chains, television was rearing its gap-toothed head, and an atmosphere of unease had settled over the industry. No one was more uneasy than the British.

And with good reason. I said before that there was no shortage of British colonies around the world, but that was prewar thinking. By '48, India was out of the empire and a line had formed at the exit. The idea of empire was out of fashion, along with movies celebrating it, so Hollywood's British Colony was looking for the sun to set in a big way.

They couldn't have asked for a better swan song than *The Tempest*, which, from what I'd been told, had been Shakespeare's own farewell piece. The aptness of it alone had me pulling for this movie. But then I almost always pulled for a movie.

Paddy, who had a less sentimental view of the industry, consulted his pocket watch after some serious squirming in his chair. "Time to meet our latest suitor," he said.

TWO

I couldn't actually serve up Shakespearean plot summaries on command. Not even on Paddy's command. Between the time I'd first heard of the *Tempest* job and our trip to Arcadia, I'd done a little research.

It had started out as an evening of dancing with my fiancée, Ella. We'd gone to the Palladium on Sunset, a place that referred to itself as a "ballroom-café" in its ads. Only in Hollywood could a barn with seating for a thousand be called a "café." The kidney-shaped and cork-padded dance floor held seven thousand in a pinch, which showed what the management thought of its cooking. They'd needed that kind of space during the war, when servicemen on leave and defense plant workers on a tear had strained the Hollywood dance clubs.

There was nothing like that big a crowd on the night of my

Tempest refresher course, not even with Glen Gray and his boys on the bandstand. But that was fine with Ella and me.

Dancing with Ella was as effortless as the perfect golf swing. She was a summertime blonde with eyes only a half shade bluer than the Palladium's chromium decor. A publicist for Warner Bros., Ella had a contact in the wardrobe department who lent her the odd evening gown. Tonight's number was coral, the same color as the ballroom's pinstripes, perhaps not coincidentally. In addition to being the right color, the gown was breathtakingly tight, which should have restricted Ella's movements but didn't. In fact, she moved so perfectly to the set-closing rumba that I suspected the band members were taking the beat from her bottom and not Gray's baton. I couldn't say I blamed them.

Back at our table, I sipped at a neglected Gibson while Ella waxed rhapsodic over Shakespeare's own set closer, *The Tempest*. She'd already given me the bare bones of the plot. Now I was in for the critical perspective.

"You really should read it, Scotty. It's a nearly perfect play. I mean, except for the masque in the next to the last act."

"The what?"

"The masque. A sort of play within the play. A masque was a kind of Elizabethan revue. Prospero conjures up a little one toward the end of *The Tempest* as an entertainment for Miranda and Ferdinand, the two lovers. This particular masque is a celebration of love and fertility."

"Fertility? Maybe I will have to read this thing."

Ella ignored me, pointedly. "The masque's okay, but it kind of interrupts the play's momentum, like the musical numbers in a Marx Brothers' movie."

"They put those in so high school kids can neck." I had

necking on the brain just then. I thought Ella might, too, based on the way she'd been wiggling on the dance floor. "Maybe Shakespeare was just being thoughtful."

"He was being profound. With *The Tempest*, I mean. It was the last play of the greatest playwright who ever lived. You're not a writer, Scotty, but you used to be an actor. Imagine yourself in the part. In Shakespeare's place. You'd want your last play to be a distillation of everything you believed. And everything you'd learned about how to write a play. *The Tempest* is all of that. Even the verse is so pure and transparent it's almost prose."

She stopped then and gazed deeply into my eyes, searching for some spark kindled by her enthusiasm.

I read her mind out loud. "Why am I marrying this big galoot whose idea of high culture is a Greer Garson double feature?"

Ella pushed back her chair. "Take me home and I'll show you a double feature. It may give you some idea why I'm marrying you."

Ella's home was a little apartment in Burbank decorated in very modern objects d'art, some with accent pillows. We had an undress rehearsal for our honeymoon, following which Ella curled up and went to sleep, as was her habit. I slipped out into her little parlor for a Lucky Strike, as was my habit.

There, in a bookcase whose sides were unmatched rhomboids, I found a paperback copy of *The Tempest*. I sat down to read a cigarette's worth of the thing and ended up finishing it.

I almost woke Ella to tell her that she was right about the

play. But I didn't. There was no point in shaking up her view of me so close to the rice throwing.

THREE

The racetrack's air-conditioned clubhouse was very nice. So was the reception we got, with one white-jacketed waiter holding the door open for us and another practically bowing double as he led us inside.

"I don't know why it is," Paddy said, "but I always get treated like royalty at a racetrack."

"They're probably mistaking you for Pat O'Brien," I said, naming the actor Paddy somewhat resembled. "Didn't he and Bing Crosby own the Del Mar track?"

"Crosby had some serious money in it. O'Brien was mostly a beard." Then, Paddy's opinion of my street savvy being similar to Ella's of my formal education, he explained the term for me. "You know, a guy who fronts for the real money men."

By then the bobbing waiter had delivered us to our table.

I'd never met the guy seated there, but I'd seen him often enough, mostly before the war, when he'd been pointed out to me in various nightspots. His name was Joel Jeffries, and, back then, he'd been an assistant to David O. Selznick. He was a dark, intense looking guy with more hair than seemed reasonable. He wore it brushed straight back and piled high, perhaps to give himself a little more height, which he badly needed, a fact I remembered about him when he stood up to shake our hands.

"Thanks for being willing to meet me way out here, Mr. Maguire."

Paddy made light of that and then introduced me, which turned out not to be necessary. Evidently I'd been pointed out to Jeffries back when he'd been pointed out to me.

"I remember you, Mr. Elliott. You were at Paramount, right? May I call you Scott? We're members of the same club, after all. The displaced war veterans of Hollywood."

Jeffries was referring to a previous incarnation of mine, the acting career Ella had mentioned in passing at the Palladium. Prior to getting myself drafted in 1941, I'd been a contract player. For Paramount, as Jeffries had correctly remembered. After my discharge, I'd been just another has-been looking for a job. The same thing had happened to Jeffries, as he now explained succinctly.

"I went into the navy after Pearl Harbor and ended up on the beach."

"Selznick didn't welcome you back?" Paddy asked solicitously.

"Promised me the next opening that came up. I'm still waiting for it to open. That's okay. His assistants are glorified stenographers anyway. Delegation's not exactly David's strong suit. I'd have had to leave him sooner or later if I wanted to produce. Now I've got my chance. That is, I'll have it if you guys can pull me out of a jam."

"That's our strong suit," Paddy said.

He wasn't bragging, either. Pulling out was a Hollywood Security specialty. Also hushing up, paying off, and leaning on. A strange job for an ex-actor, you might say, but then I was also an ex-artilleryman. After you'd spent a few months lobbing howitzer shells at strangers and having them lob a few back at you, everything else, even peeping through keyholes for a living, seemed pretty normal.

"You may have heard about the *Tempest* production I'm putting together," Jeffries said with a modesty that must have come in handy around Selznick.

"A fine idea," Paddy said, though he might have been referring to the Tom Collins that the waiter had brought him at a signal from Jeffries. He cleared things up a little by adding, "I've always been partial to the Bard's romances."

"Shakespeare's hot right now. Larry Olivier's *Hamlet* is getting some fine press, better even than that *Henry V* he did a couple years back. And Ronald Colman just won an Oscar for doing a couple of scenes from *Othello* in *A Double Life*."

I thought he'd gotten the statue for strangling Shelley Winters, but I didn't have a chance to interject.

Paddy was saying, "I hear Colman's your pick for Prospero, the deposed duke turned magician."

"He'll be perfect in the part. And he's interested. He's even let his name be linked with the project in the columns as a way of testing the water. That was a personal favor to me. I met him back when Selznick did *The Prisoner of Zenda*.

But Colman hasn't signed a contract yet."

"Who else are you thinking about?" I asked.

"Joan Fontaine for Miranda. She's a little old, I know, but the whole cast is skewed a little that way. The British Colony veterans are all, well, veterans. Like Cedric Hardwicke, who I'm hoping will play our king, Alonso, and Basil Rathbone. I'm going to lure him back from Broadway to play Sebastian, Hardwicke's evil brother. Henry Daniell is interested in Antonio, Prospero's equally evil brother. I think Daniell and Rathbone will make a great pair of schemers. I'd like Herbert Marshall for Gonzalo, the king's wise old counselor. Ian Hunter would also work, but I'd prefer Marshall. Caliban, the monster, will be my real coup—after landing Colman, of course. I'm in negotiation with Boris Karloff. He's a little old, like the rest of them, but once he's in the makeup I have in mind, nobody will notice. For Ariel, the sprite, I'm thinking of Charles Laughton's wife, Elsa Lanchester. It's not a woman's part, but we could use another one in the cast, and she could give the thing an offbeat, comic twist."

Jeffries had gone from chatting with us to pitching his movie, his dark eyes alight and his right hand squeezing his empty glass so tightly I was ready to dodge shrapnel. I found myself wishing, for Jeffries's sake, that Ella was there to return his enthusiasm.

Paddy, who'd been around long enough to know that every rotten movie had once been somebody's dream child, merely smiled politely and asked, "What about the juvenile lead, Ferdinand? You've not mentioned him."

The light went out of Jeffries's eyes, and I knew we were getting down to business at last.

"I wanted Richard Ney, but he's not available, so I've

signed Forrest Combs."

I'd never met Combs, but I knew his work. He'd hit town around 1940, when the studios had been cranking out pro-British propaganda and needed men the right age and with the right accents to pilot their cardboard Spitfires.

"He's no Olivier," Paddy conceded, "but he should do fine. Or will he?"

"Oh, he can handle the part," Jeffries said. "It's not that." He signaled for another round. As a further stall, he actually leaned across and lit the cigar Paddy had pulled from his jacket pocket. By then my interest was piqued but good.

"We're at a very delicate stage in our negotiations. Some of these old-timers, Colman and Hardwicke, for example, are very sensitive about their reputations. They don't want to be associated with anything low budget or thrown together. They certainly don't want anything to do with a scandal."

"A scandal you say?" Paddy's curiosity was piqued now, too.

Jeffries was leaning across the table again. "It's no big deal really," he said, contradicting himself by whispering. "I've heard from a friendly columnist that Forrest Combs is seeing someone."

"A male or female someone?" Paddy asked.

"Definitely female."

"And Combs is married?"

"No. That's not the problem. It's the woman. She's a, a ..."

Paddy wasn't much for parlor games. "A what? A Commie spy? A dognapper? A politician?"

Jeffries sighed. "A burlesque queen. Her name is Betty Ann Baker."

Paddy whistled. "The farmer's daughter herself. I'll say this for Combs, he doesn't believe in half measures."

Stage shows featuring more or less undressed women were an institution in Hollywood. Earl Carroll's Vanities and the big productions at the Florentine Gardens, to name just two, dated from the thirties. But it had taken the wartime flood of GIs to establish a true burlesque tradition in staid Los Angeles. Ken Murray, a former Earl Carroll headliner, had taken a long step that way with his "Backouts," which starred a professional dumb blonde named Marie Wilson. Murray's shows had been topped in turn by the genuine burlesque houses, like the Avalon Club and the Casa Rose.

Baker was the house blonde at the Avalon. Her nickname, "the farmer's daughter," came from the part she played in a series of risqué skits that ran between the dance numbers.

"A girl from the chorus we might be able to keep quiet," Jeffries muttered to the tabletop. "But not Betty Ann Baker. These days her name's in the paper more often than Truman's. If it gets linked in print just once with Combs's, Colman and the rest of the old-school-tie boys will stop taking my calls."

Paddy brushed cigar ash from his no-school tie and said, "So replace Combs."

"I can't. He's signed a contract. He's the only one who has signed so far. The day before the call about Baker came in. Talk about bad timing."

"Can the columnist who tipped you be trusted to sit on this?" I asked.

Jeffries was genuinely unconcerned. "Don't worry about him. Combs is the problem. I need you to break this Baker thing up. Or at least hush it up until we've started shooting.

If you can do that, I'll be in your debt."

They were my boss's favorite words, but still he played coy. "Shouldn't Combs get his orders straight from you?"

"I've already talked with him. He won't listen. Almost punched me in the nose for suggesting that this affair is only an affair. He thinks it's the first true love to hit this town since Pickford dumped Fairbanks.

"Forget Combs. The thing can only be worked through Baker. That's why I need you guys. I can't afford to be seen with her any more than Combs can. And nobody can know you're working for me. That's why I insisted on meeting you out here."

"It may mean some money changing hands," Paddy observed.

Jeffries took a pen from his pocket and wrote a figure on a damp cocktail napkin. I counted three zeros when he pushed it across to Paddy.

"Promise her that much to forget she ever met Combs. And a second payment the day we finish shooting."

Paddy tucked the napkin into his watch pocket. "Consider it done," he said.

FOUR

A handshake later Paddy and I were on our way back to Hollywood in my 1948 Nash convertible, one of a limited run of convertibles in their Ambassador line. It was a streamlined maroon beauty with a double front grille, a little one over a wheel-to-wheel one, both made up entirely of horizontal bands of chrome. The stylized hood ornament also had a backup. Beneath it was a badge displaying the Nash coat of arms. The badge had caused Paddy to wryly observe that, in America, only the cars had bloodlines. But then, he didn't think a detective should drive anything flashier than a flivver. Me, I would have sprung for the Packard convertible Nash was imitating with the Ambassador, if I hadn't been saving up for married life.

We hadn't driven very far before Paddy observed, "I smell a fish."

I knew he was speaking, metaphorically, of this *Tempest* job, and I agreed. "An ancient fish."

"Can Jeffries's production really be balanced so precariously that a little slip of a girl could topple it? I wonder. Did you notice that Jeffries never once mentioned where the money for this movie was coming from? I think I'll do some asking around about it while you're talking to Combs."

"Combs? Jeffries said to go after Baker."

"Since when does a client fill out our dance card? We'd best start off by verifying Jeffries's story, and that includes getting Combs's version of this romance. Besides, the Combs residence will be a lot easier to find than Betty Ann Baker's. I doubt she's in the phone book. We know she'll be at the Avalon Club, but probably not till tonight. So you've time to kill."

"You're sending me to a burlesque house two nights before my wedding?"

Paddy's booming laugh was genuine, telling me he'd forgotten how sensitive the timing was. "Think of it as your bachelor party. You were cheated out of one when that best man of yours got sauced and fell off his train. Take Ella along for company, if you like. I'd go myself, but there's a little something I promised I'd attend to for Lana Turner."

"Just remember that one of us is already married," I said, and Paddy laughed again.

Forrest Combs wasn't in the phone book either, as it turned out. But he was easy enough to trace through the Screen Actors Guild. My contact there sent me up to Mulholland Drive, the road that snaked along the crest of the Santa Monica Mountains.

Combs's house was a modest ranch, but it had a million dollar view. Or views. To the north was little Tarzana and beyond it the lush San Fernando Valley. To the south was glittering Santa Monica Bay, with Los Angeles on one side and the Pacific on the other.

I didn't bother ringing the doorbell. As I'd parked in the half-moon drive behind a Plymouth DeLuxe, I'd noticed a tennis court protected by a windscreen of stunted cypress. I would have heard the court if I hadn't seen it. Once I'd shut the Nash down, the pok pok of the current volley came through loud and clear. I ambled that way, took a seat on a bench that was angled for the bay view, and lit a Lucky.

From there I could see one end of the court and the back of a six-foot man with blond hair who moved like a skinny Bill Tilden. It was Combs, or his stand-in. I identified him positively as the actor when he chased a missed shot my way. He flipped the loose ball up with his racquet, caught it, and saw me.

He might have stood there staring for the duration of my cigarette, if his partner hadn't called out to him. Combs gave himself a little shake and then marched out of my view. I made a point of seeing the other player as Combs led the way to the drive, but it wasn't a burlesque dancer or even a she. A tennis pro who made house calls, I deduced, and that seemed to be confirmed when Combs reached for his wallet as they neared the Plymouth. A minute later the car was gone and Combs was coming my way.

I stood up, a little puzzled. I didn't think I looked like the kind of heavy who goes house-to-house telling guys to lay off runway queens. So I couldn't understand why Combs hadn't taken the logical step of asking me my business before he'd cut his lesson short.

He addressed my unspoken question when he got within a few feet of me. "I was told you'd be coming."

"Who by?" I might just as easily have said, "By whom?" But there was something about Combs's too genteel English accent that made me want to take the low road.

"By the woman you've come here to defame. She's a little more worldly than I am. She knows how these matters are handled."

I almost asked him how she had come by her extensive knowledge of these matters, but that might have ended with one of us on the grass.

"Let's start over," I said. "My name's—"

"I don't want to know your name," Combs replied, his voice trembling a little. I remembered then that, in his wartime films, he often played the member of the squadron or platoon who cracked under pressure.

"Just get in your car and go. And tell Joel Jeffries that I won't be intimidated."

I shrugged and started for the Nash, Combs a step behind me, if that. He followed so closely I thought he might be planning to help me along with a hand on my collar. Luckily for the peace of the afternoon, he didn't.

At the drive, I turned and forced him back a step with a question. "Why don't you just tear up your contract with Jeffries? Then he'd relax and you'd be free to do as you please."

Combs had delicate, almost feminine features, which was another thing that qualified him to play the company weakling. Right now, though, what jaw he had was firmly set.

"Give up the first decent part I've ever been offered? My

chance to work with actors I've admired all my life? My boyhood heroes? Why not ask me to give up the world?"

"The choice is between the part and a woman," I said, "not the world."

"The woman *is* my world," Combs shot back, which I'd more or less asked for. As corny as the line was, it tugged me a little way toward Combs's side of things.

"I won't give her up. And I won't give up a role that could justify the years I've wasted in this town. Tell Jeffries that. And tell him, if he should try to use some morals clause in my contract to drop me, I'll raise such a stink in the newspapers the whole movie will go down with me. Tell him that."

"I will." I was behind the wheel of the Nash by then. "If you'll do two things for me."

"What things?"

"First, take my card. You don't have to look at it. Just keep it handy in case you decide you want to talk. I'll put my home number on the back."

Combs watched me do it and then took the card. "What's the second thing?"

"Answer a question for me." I'd remembered an observation Ella had once made, namely that couples in love can't resist telling everyone how they'd first gotten together. Combs's feelings seemed pretty genuine, but then he was an actor. So I tried the Ella test. "Where did you and Miss Baker meet?"

Combs had been screwing himself up to tell me to stuff my question until he actually heard it. Then he laughed.

"In a public library," he said.

FIVE

I took Paddy's suggestion and asked Ella to go with me to the Avalon Club, hoping the invitation would convince her that the visit was totally innocent. I was sure she wouldn't accept, so naturally she did.

We got there a little late, as the invitation had gotten stretched to include dinner and Ella didn't trust the Avalon's kitchen. We made it a quick one at the Brown Derby, but it was still after nine before we were in our seats near the Avalon's runway.

Those seats were at a little table, the Avalon being set up as a nightclub rather than a theater. Ella was dressed somewhat conservatively tonight, in a dark blue suit whose very short jacket buttoned at the neck and only there, giving her chest room to expand. That chest was covered by a white silk blouse that buttoned more comprehensively than the jacket, but Ella had still drawn her share of admiring glances as we'd entered.

"So nice to feel welcome," she'd whispered in my ear.

We suffered through a chorus number, the perpetrators of which were dressed as cowgirls, though dressed is overstating it, as their costumes consisted largely of gun belts and hats and strategically placed stars. That was followed by a blackout skit featuring the woman we'd come to see, in the role that had made her famous.

The crowd was applauding as soon as the curtain opened to reveal the farmhouse set and the baggy-pants comedian with the salesman's case who was knocking on its front door. Things settled a little during the obligatory banter between the salesman comic and a farmer comic who should have been paying Walter Brennan royalties. The audience cut loose again when Baker made her entrance in bib overalls, cut off at the hip, and a smile. She wore her golden hair in a loose cascade, like Al Capp's Daisy Mae, whom she more than somewhat resembled.

All the noise made it hard to follow the plot of the thing, but I gathered that it hadn't been adapted from Shakespeare. It ended in a well worn haystack, with Baker almost managing to hold up the bib of her overalls with one delicate hand.

I stood during the ovation that followed the blackout. "Might as well strike while the iron is hot, so to speak," I shouted to Ella.

"Good idea," she shouted back. "Catch her with her pants down, so to speak. I'm coming with you."

I thought about it and agreed. If I'd left Ella there unattended, the waiters would have gotten bow-legged from lugging over her free drinks.

The route backstage was busy with outbound traffic. Evidently the chorus girls were permitted, and possibly encouraged, to fraternize with the drink-buying customers. Ordinarily I would have run interference for Ella in a crowded corridor. In this particular crowd, she blocked for me.

As a result, Ella encountered the obstacle first. It took the form of a swarthy guy dressed in one of George Raft's old double-breasted tuxedoes.

"Hold it, sister," he said. "No auditions during a show. Come back Thursday."

"I'm getting married Thursday," Ella said. "How about Friday?"

By then, the bouncer had noticed me and I had recognized him. "You're Lubos Torrealba, aren't you?"

"That's right," he said and flashed us a smile with a fair amount of gold in it. Nobody really appreciates being recognized until it stops happening regularly, as I knew all too well. Torrealba had been a promising middleweight, once upon a time.

"I think I dropped a sawbuck on you once," I said.

Torrealba rubbed an old scar above his right eye. "I hear that a lot. What can I do for you folks?"

"I'd like to see Miss Baker. My fiancée here needs a quiet place to sit."

"Congrats," Torrealba said, connecting the fiancée tag with Ella's earlier remark about Thursday's big event. He might have been marked up, but he wasn't punchy. "Is Miss Baker expecting you?"

"Sort of." If she'd foreseen my visit to Combs, she would certainly be expecting this next step. "Tell her it's a man about a movie."

"That line's been tried," Torrealba began. Then he remembered Ella, who was smiling brightly at his elbow. "I'll tell her. You can wait back here out of the traffic."

He led us to the intersection of two hallways. One passage contained dressing rooms, most of them open and noisy. The other hall was quieter and ended in a door marked "private."

While we were waiting, that private door opened and two men came out. The first was a standard issue bodyguard, probably an ex-pug like Torrealba. The second was a prominent member of the local syndicate, the name the papers liked for the organization that ran the surviving gambling joints. His name was Tip Fasano.

I didn't want Fasano to place me, so I gathered Ella up and gave her the kind of kiss that usually precedes the closing credits. I heard Fasano chuckle as he and his escort passed, but that was all.

When it was safe to breathe again, Ella said, "Getting it all out of your system before you go in to see Betty Ann?"

"Something like that. While I'm in there, keep an eye on that door at the end of the hall. And fix your lipstick."

Torrealba was coming back, getting his hair mussed as he wove his way through chorines in sailor hats and gauzy jumpers.

"You're in," he said to me.

SIX

Paddy had called Betty Ann Baker "a little slip of a girl," which was about as accurate as calling Jimmy Durante "moderately outgoing." She was posing when I entered her dressing room, but then women of her height, easily five nine, and build were posing most of the time, whether they wanted to be or not. She had taken her stand in front of a full-length mirror, but she was facing the door and me, wearing heels and a silk dressing gown whose color was rose, a pale rose on her broad sunlit uplands and a dusky rose below. It was cinched tightly at her wasp waist, to emphasize that feature, probably. Everywhere else, the robe was unsupervised and indiscreet.

The natural thing in Hollywood, when you met someone even halfway good looking, was to wonder why they weren't in pictures. In the case of Baker, who was actually striking, the answer might have been that she personified the phrase "too much of a good thing." Or maybe not. Hollywood had spent years, after all, establishing the illusion that statuesque was the national average. The trouble might have been the jarring contrast between her body and her face. Her features were as delicate as Combs's and all but lost against the golden hair.

Of course, the most likely problem area was her voice. On stage, she'd belted out her lines in a twang as broad as the comedy. I waited with a touch of anxiety to hear the real thing. When she finally delivered, her "What can I do for you?" came out in a voice so soft and husky it hit me like what Paddy called "the old sleeve across the windpipe."

I didn't answer right away, and she was a little nervous, so she spoke again. "I was expecting someone shadier. That's the way you struck Forrest this afternoon."

"I've had a shoe shine since then," I managed to say.

"Been to college, too," Baker observed. "You are the guy, aren't you?"

"I'm the guy. I'm here to ask you to lay off Combs. For the time being, at least."

Baker must have been tired of arching her back. She took a seat at her dressing table, nodding me toward a chaise lounge that probably had more stories to tell than my boss. I settled very lightly on its edge.

"Ask me?" Baker repeated. "Or order me?"

"Ask," I said. "Politely."

"You think it's ever polite to offer a lady money? You're ready to buy me off, aren't you?" She leaned forward to get a better look at me. "Are you blushing? Did I embarrass you by mentioning the dough? Buddy, are you ever in the wrong business."

I was blushing but good by then, because I was there to offer her money, because I was in the wrong business, and because her forward posture had caused her robe to gape like the Golden Gate. "Would offering you money do any good?"

Baker settled back. "Thanks for not throwing the lady claim in my face. A shady guy would have. And no, nothing you have to offer me will do you any good, so you can push off right now."

I might have, if I hadn't been genuinely curious. "What's a few months to Combs and you?"

"My experience with men is, a few days can make a difference," Baker said, but she didn't put much into it. She was pushing things around on her dressing table and looking wounded. I felt as though I had thrown the lady claim in her face.

"You okay?"

"Sure, I'm great. I'm a leper, but what's that to a girl with nice legs? So what if I can kill a movie just by dating a guy who's in it?"

"Not any movie. Only one being made by stuffed shirts for other stuffed shirts."

She swung around to face me. "Only a film version of the greatest play ever written, you mean. A movie that's going to be around a long time after we're both dead."

I almost called out for Ella, weakly. "You're a fan of *The Tempest*?"

"Only since Forrest's been talking it up." She was delivering her lines to the makeup table again, and not very convincingly.

"How did you and Combs meet?" I asked by way of an intermezzo.

"At a lecture," Baker said.

"He told me a library."

The suggestion that I was questioning her word brought a little color back into her cheeks. "It was a lecture at a library. The Culver City branch. Feel free to call and check."

"It wouldn't have been a lecture on *The Tempest* by any chance."

"What if it was?"

"For one thing, it would mean you were interested in the play before Combs mentioned it to you."

"So what? So I read in the trades that they were making a movie and I saw a lecture in the *Times* and I went. Is there a law against dreaming? You think I want to be rolling around in some flea-trap haystack the rest of my life?"

I felt a second figurative blow to my windpipe. I'd started off wondering, idly, why Baker wasn't in pictures, and now it turned out she was wondering the same thing herself. And not about pictures in general.

"You went to that lecture because you were hoping to test for *The Tempest*?"

"Test?" She was fingering a hairbrush in a threatening manner. "Is Ronald Colman making a screen test? What makes you think I'd have to? Maybe I've got connections, wise guy. Maybe I can just ask for a part and get it."

"Combs doesn't have that kind of pull. He'll be lucky to hang on to his own part."

"Who said anything about Forrest?" Baker snapped and then caught herself. She'd said too much, evidently. "Get out now. I've got to get undressed for my next bit."

I got as far as the door and stopped. I had a soft spot for long shots, and I'd never heard of a longer shot than the one Baker was betting on.

"Look," I said. "There's nothing wrong with dreaming, but don't waste too much of it on this *Tempest* movie. The guy behind it isn't the type to take a gamble."

Baker, her back to me, was using the threatening hairbrush on her golden mane. "If you mean Joel Jeffries, he's not behind the picture. He's in front of it. And he may not be there for long, not if he makes it a choice between him and Forrest. Or him and me."

SEVEN

Ella was at her post. "Well?" she asked, her smile a little stiff. "Are you under her spell?"

"Sorry," I said. "Have we met? My past life's a blur."

She was smiling now for real. "Your future's hazy, too, fellah. What are we doing next?"

I pondered. My impulse was to find a quiet place to think and drink. Baker had given me enough thinking material to last through a pitcher of Gibsons, notably the teaser about Joel Jeffries being a front for the real producer of *The Tempest*. A beard, to use the gambler's term Paddy had mentioned just that afternoon. Thinking of that expression reminded me that I'd seen a gambler very recently, Tip Fasano. If Baker was right, if Jeffries was just protective cover, Fasano might be the real money man. Then again, Baker's influential friend could be a lot closer, as close as the door at the end of the hall.

I indicated the door to Ella. "Any action down that way?"

"Yes. Just after you left, a little bald guy popped out and started bawling for Torrealba. The two of them went inside and shut the door. Then he — Torrealba — came out carrying a box. A heavy box."

"Big enough for a body?"

"Just for the head."

"Too bad." Still, a lead was a lead. I took Ella by the arm and headed for the quiet part of the neighborhood. I knocked quietly, too, not wanting to attract the absent Torrealba. The answering "Yes?" was also soft. Soft and, I thought, sad.

Inside we found the little guy Ella had mentioned, seated behind a desk. He was wearing a boiled shirt and a black bow tie. The tuxedo jacket that went with the outfit hung on the chair behind him. He had a lot of head above his ears, most of it hairless, dark eyes, and a long nose that was bulbed at the end. The nose was also red, maybe from blowing, maybe from drinking. There was evidence on the desktop to support either guess: a crumpled handkerchief on one side and a bottle of scotch and a glass on the other. Between those two exhibits was spread a hand of solitaire.

"You the folks who stopped by to see Betty Ann?" the little guy asked in an English accent almost as genteel as Combs's. It would have been every bit as good but for a slight slurring that was probably the work of the scotch. "Lubos mentioned you. I'm Ian Kendall, by the way. I own this palace."

He said the last part ruefully, which is how you would expect a gentleman to deliver the news that he owned a burlesque house.

I introduced myself and my fiancée, who had strayed to an

oil painting that hung on a spotlit wall. The picture showed piebald cows dining.

"Is this a Constable?" Ella asked.

"Just a copy," Kendall said, a little quickly. "You've quite the eye."

My own eye had been drawn to a bookcase beneath the painting. It contained works by the great English novelists and playwrights, with the interesting exception of William Shakespeare. However, there was a notable gap in the center of the topmost shelf. And something else was missing from the case. On the very top, near where Ella stood admiring the cows, a six-inch circle of clean wood stood out clearly against the general dustiness. Something had recently stood there, something round or with a round base.

Kendall had gathered up his cards and was shuffling them with casual skill. He'd yet to ask us our business, but he came close to doing it now.

"Was Betty Ann able to help you?"

"Not really," I said. "Maybe you can. If you have any influence with her."

"I discovered her." He did a chemmy shuffle across the desktop, spreading out the cards and gathering them up again. "She was working in a bowling alley in Maywood, can you believe it? I knew right away that she was destined for bigger—if not better—things. Since then I've grown quite fond of her. She's like a—" He coughed. "We're good friends."

He fanned deck and held it out to Ella. "Pick a card."

She did and showed it to me. The six of clubs.

"Stick it back in anywhere," Kendall said. "I promise not to peek."

After she had, he returned to shuffling. I said, "Would

Baker lay off a guy if you asked her to?"

"I don't know. That sounds a little personal. Someone she shouldn't know?" He cut the cards, holding one up for Ella to identify. The jack of spades.

"Nope," Ella said.

"Oops. It wouldn't be a guy like that, would it?" Kendall said as he shuffled some more. "A guy Betty shouldn't know. It would have to be the other way around. Somebody who shouldn't know her. We get a lot of that in our business. I'd have more friends if I were a mortician." He was smiling, but the dark eyes were wincing. "May I ask if you two are this unnamed gentleman's family? Friends?"

"Something in between," I said. I'd been wrestling with the idea of mentioning *The Tempest* to Kendall, just to get his reaction. Doing so would have violated Jeffries's orders and Paddy's, but that wasn't why I held back. I was suddenly sure, looking into those sad dark eyes, that the little man knew more about the movie than I did.

He cut the deck again, this time at the seven of hearts.

"Close," Ella said.

"Just not my night. Look, you seem like good people. I'll have a word with Betty."

"Thanks," I said.

"Don't mention it." He opened a desk drawer. "Take a couple of free passes, good anytime."

He handed the ducats to Ella, who started to put them in her purse. Then she stopped and separated them. The six of clubs fluttered down onto the desktop.

"Wow," she said.

Kendall beamed. "One can't do better than wow. Thank you for stopping in."

EIGHT

When we were out in the hallway again, Ella said, "If that Constable's a copy, I'm Zazu Pitts. Kendall's a sweet little guy, though. Something's hurt him tonight."

"Him and my head. When Torrealba came out with that box, which way did he go?"

"Thataway, pardner." She pointed toward dressing room row. "I didn't see exactly where. I was ordered to watch the office."

We walked back to the intersection where Ella had been standing. I could see from there that the dressing room hallway ended at a fire door. Before we could see more than that, Torrealba found us.

"Leaving?" he said in a way that barely ended in a question mark.

"Yes," I said, and Ella added, "But it's been lovely."

"Good luck at the altar."

We went out the way we'd come in. After I'd unchecked my hat, I asked Ella to wait in the Nash, politely. She laughed at me, unpolitely. Together we found the alley that led back to the fire door we'd spotted before our welcome had run out. Being well stocked with trash cans, the alley wasn't entirely uninhabited. Ella was soon regretting her decision to tag along.

"What was that?" she asked, tightening her grip on my arm.

"Ground squirrel," I said. "Or a distant relation." I started opening cans as quietly as I could.

"What are you looking for, the box? I don't think Torrealba came out here. I would have smelled this marvelous aroma."

Evidently he hadn't gone out, since there was no likely box. The fire door wouldn't open from our side. That left making my report.

I offered to take Ella home, but she was fine again as soon as we were out of the alley. So I drove us to the little bungalow where Paddy lived with his wife and business partner, Peggy.

It was the same place they'd lived in back when I'd met Paddy in the late thirties. He'd been a humble studio guard then. Now he was a guy the studio guards waved through their gates without a question, but he still slept in the same little house.

That was Peggy's influence at work. A small dark woman whose closest actress look-alike was Mildred Natwick, Peggy remembered the Great Depression and maybe one or two before that. Any money she could get away from her husband she stashed somewhere safe, a place Paddy referred to as her "coffee can."

Peggy had a soft spot for me and another, more recently developed, for Ella. She ushered us in, though the hour was getting on. Paddy was back from whatever little job he'd done for Lana Turner, if in fact he'd gone out at all. He and Ella and I sat at the kitchen table while Peggy bustled about making bacon and eggs.

Mrs. Maguire also distracted Ella with questions about the wedding preparations. I'd been excluded from any such conversation since the day I'd mistakenly said "The Wedding March" came at the beginning of the ceremony instead of at the end, so I was free to make my report to Paddy.

He took my failure with Combs okay, since that had been mostly a fishing expedition. But he didn't like the actor's threat to sink the movie. "Very unprofessional that" was how he summed up his feelings.

Likewise, his opinion of Betty Ann Baker dropped when I told him she wouldn't talk money. Her aspirations for a part in *The Tempest* had him scratching his graying head.

"Can she be that dumb?" he asked. "Can anyone?"

"You haven't heard the best part yet. Baker claims to have some secret pull."

"That's more like it." Paddy believed in secret pull, in influence, in fixes. He thought that stuff explained the workings of the universe, or at least the little corner of it called Hollywood.

"She as much as said that Jeffries is a front and that she knows the real man behind *The Tempest*."

"Every producer's a front," Paddy said, getting philosophical on me. "If they had to risk their own money, this town would be quieter than Walla Walla. But it's interesting she'd say that. I'm having a hard time tracing Jeffries's investors. Did Miss Baker name any names?"

"No, but I've got a couple to run by you." I told him of seeing Tip Fasano at the Avalon.

It didn't go over big. "Might have dropped in to see the show or to collect a marker. I don't see that character throwing hard-earned tinsel at a movie. Starry-eyed he ain't."

"Suppose his eyes are full of Betty Ann Baker?" I asked, drawing a disapproving cluck from the cook.

For her benefit, Paddy said, "Love does work wonders on a man. But if Fasano and Baker are that serious, where does Combs come in? No, that fish is all bones. Who else do you have?"

"Ian Kendall, owner of the Avalon. He came close to telling us that Baker's like a daughter to him. And he was nervous about seeing us. I think he was afraid we'd make the connection between him and the picture."

"Kendall?" Paddy, exasperated, looked up from the job of pouring catsup on his eggs, letting half the bottle run out on his plate. "That makes the Fasano angle look as straight as a new pin. If Kendall's the secret money man, why would he let Jeffries hire us to nose around and figure things out? That's risking the whole set-up, movie and all. If Colman and his cronies would back out over a costar dating beneath him, think of what they'd do if they knew the movie's being funded by some musical anatomy classes."

"Mind your language," Peggy said as she whisked away the catsup omelet.

Ella, who'd had her fill of wedding talk, took a shot at answering that. "Kendall didn't know Jeffries was going to hire you. Jeffries told you he found out about Combs and Baker from a columnist. He must have acted without orders."

Paddy was extra patient with Ella. "It won't wash, kiddo. Jeffries must know who's signing the checks. He'd never send us near Baker if there was a chance she'd lead us to Kendall. Plus there's all the coincidences. Kendall secretly financing a movie that happens to star a guy who happens to fall for Kendall's top blonde. I hate coincidences."

We kicked it around until Ella mentioned that she had to be at her desk in a few hours. Then Paddy walked us to the front door, scratching his head again.

"Seems I remember this Ian Kendall's name being whispered in some unpleasant context a few years back. Can't quite remember."

"Aid for England," Peggy called out from the kitchen.

"That's it. You kids remember Aid for England, don't you? Raised a pot of money to help out over there during the blitz and after."

"What did Kendall have to do with that?" I asked.

"Something back office. Then he got the heave-ho. It was hushed up so the givers wouldn't stop giving, but I think it had something to do with some money going missing."

Ella, who'd been yawning for all of us, was suddenly wide awake. "Wasn't Aid For England the pet charity of the British Colony?"

"It was," said Peggy, who'd joined us on the front steps. "Basil Rathbone was president of the California chapter. And Ronald Colman was involved."

"All of them were," Ella said. "All of the guys who are supposed to be making *The Tempest*."

"I hate coincidences," Paddy said again.

NINE

Ella decided we should spend the night apart, to create a little suspense for the honeymoon. I left her at her building's elevator with a kiss and a question.

"Know any tame columnists?"

"There's no such thing," she said. "The best of them would trade his mother's wooden leg for a story."

"That's what I thought. But Jeffries wasn't a bit worried that the columnist who tipped him might use the Combs item."

"Then he's nuts," Ella said, speaking around another yawn.

"I was wondering if there's a safe way to check Jeffries's story, to find out if he really was tipped by a sob sister."

"You mean without handing the bombshell story to every newspaper in town?"

"I do."

Ella got a dreamy look on her face. "I love the way you deliver that line."

"Focus."

"I've a favor or two I can call in. Leave it to me."

In anticipation of married life, I'd given up my little cottage in the hills—the shack where I'd lived rent-free since my discharge—and taken a good-size apartment in Glendale. I'd no sooner gotten the door of the place unlocked than the phone began to ring. Ella calling to tell me to sleep well, I thought, incorrectly.

"You bastard!" the caller said. The male caller. The English-accented male caller. Forrest Combs, possibly drunk. "Damn you for interfering with my life. With our life."

"What? What's happened?" My first guess was that Jeffries had taken Paddy's advice and tossed Combs. The second mistake of my current series.

"She's broken if off. Betty Ann. She said she can't see me again. Said it was for my own good. My own good."

"When I left her, she was in your corner." Of course, I'd immediately run to her boss and asked him to apply the screws.

Combs seemed to read that afterthought. "Liar. I told you what I'd do if you ruined this for me. I'm calling the papers."

I was sure now that he was drunk. "What good would that do? Your threat made sense when you were worried about being dropped from the picture. That won't happen now. But if you start making phone calls, you'll lose the part and the girl."

"Do you think I care about a part?" Combs demanded, but I could tell his brain was in gear at last.

"Don't do anything till you sober up. Give me a chance to find out what happened. I'll call you tomorrow." I looked at my watch. "I mean, today."

I tapped down the switch hook and started to dial Paddy's number. Then I hung up altogether. If I gave Paddy the news, he'd fire off a bill to Jeffries and declare the job over. And I'd never find out what had really been going on.

TEN

By that hour, even the Avalon Club was locked up tight. Or as tight as a business whose assets had all walked out on their own tired feet needed to be locked. I decided to start in the alley where Ella and I had disturbed the animal population. The fire door we'd found there had been buttoned, but the buttons were old and lightweight. The door was wired to an alarm, too, but in the mostly-for-show way that Paddy covered in the first day of the little training course he ran for new employees. Before the rats were fully awake, I was inside, listening to the sounds of the place, the creaks and pops and sighs.

My to-do list contained exactly two items. I wanted to find the famous box that Kendall had been so anxious to have out of his office, assuming it was still around to find. And I wanted to search that office for some proof of a link between the owner and Jeffries. Paddy's objections to that link had made a world of sense, but I was more certain than ever that it existed. Someone had changed Baker's mind for her, and I was betting on Kendall. But I didn't believe he'd done it because Ella and I had made such a good first impression.

I located the box right away. The first door I came to was the janitor's closet. I clicked on my flashlight and there was a chewed-up cardboard box fitting Ella's description. She'd said it was big enough to hold a head but not a body. Having that in mind made finding a head inside a little less shocking than it would otherwise have been. That the head was made of gold-painted plaster also helped. It was a bust of William Shakespeare. I didn't lift it out to measure the base, but I was sure it would match the hole I'd seen in Kendall's dust. Likewise, I was sure the books squeezed in around the bust—a complete set of Shakespeare in blue leather—would fill the gap in the Kendall's little library.

His office was my next stop. It might have been cleaned to the wallpaper while Ella and I were having our bacon and eggs, but finding the bust and the books still on the premises gave me heart.

I lost a little of it when I determined that the office door was unlocked. No secret papers in there, I thought, but I went in anyway. That the office was windowless I knew from my first visit, so I reached for the wall switch. Reached for it and froze.

In the movies, people are always stumbling across dead bodies, literally. Lou Costello had practically made a career of being blissfully unaware of a stiff until he opened the wrong closet or pulled the wrong curtain or tripped over the wrong lump in the carpet. Then there'd be two minutes of business while he tried to say, "Hey, Abbott," or words to that effect.

In real life, dead bodies have a way of announcing themselves, usually to your nose. Even against the Avalon's distinctive odor, a combination of expensive perfume, cheap scent, and sweat, I could smell this body plainly.

I switched on the light. Ian Kendall lay on his back beneath the Constable painting, one hand on his heart, as though he'd felt some warning gurgle in his chest. Except this wasn't death by heart attack or any other natural cause. He'd been hit hard enough on the front of his bald scalp to crack the bone beneath.

Or so it seemed, based on the amount of blood around. I'd just stooped down to get a closer look and to confirm that he was dead when a floorboard creaked behind me.

I sprang up and turned, adding that much more momentum to the haymaker Lubos Torrealba was throwing. Then it was lights out.

ELEVEN

When I came to, I was the property of the Los Angeles Police Department. Torrealba had called them in after finding me crouched over his dead employer and jumping to the obvious conclusion.

Luckily, the police weren't such fast jumpers. The guy in charge, a battle-damaged war veteran named Dempsey, didn't exactly believed the tale I wove him, but he didn't haul out the rubber hose over it. My story was that Hollywood Security had been hired to break up a romance between an unnamed actor and Betty Ann Baker, hired by the concerned friends and relations of the actor. That last wrinkle had been suggested to me by a remark Kendall had made, when he'd pretended to mistake me and Ella for Combs's worried friends. I'd been at the Avalon after hours looking for any love letters the actor might have been indiscreet enough to write. In the process of which, I'd sniffed out the body and investigated, good citizen that I was.

I could have spiced up that goulash by mentioning that I'd seen Tip Fasano at the club earlier in the evening, but Paddy had taught me never to tell the police more than was necessary to preserve life and limb.

It didn't hurt my case that Kendall's blood had been drying for at least an hour at the moment Torrealba KO'd me, a fact even the boxer had recognized, though a bit too late. Still, Dempsey had more than enough to hold me on, if he wanted to hold me. I attributed my quick release to Paddy's silver tongue, but the man himself credited our past successes.

"We solved a murder for Dempsey before, after all," Paddy said when I was again breathing unconfined air. "He's probably hoping for another assist."

I wasn't surprised to hear that we'd be investigating. My earlier fear that Paddy would close the case had died with Ian Kendall. Hollywood Security was involved in a murder now, and it would be bad for business to let the proper authorities handle it.

It was noon by then. We were standing in line at a tamale vendor's cart, Paddy having thoughtfully selected soft food on account of my sore teeth. I was sore generally and anxious to have my reprimand behind me, so I said, "Sorry about the screw-up."

Paddy shrugged. "I don't mind a man showing a little initiative, especially a man who can keep his mouth shut. I take it Dempsey didn't mention Fasano because you didn't. An important omission. Maybe more important than keeping Forrest Combs out of it."

"I didn't mention him, either."

"I know. I did. Two please," this last to the tamale guy. "I had to give Dempsey something. He knew you were holding back and figured it was on my orders. He's a man who can appreciate a chain of command. And he's old school where actors are concerned. He'll keep Combs's name out of the papers if he can."

"But Combs will spill everything. He was mad enough to do it this morning."

"He's cooled a bit since then. I managed to reach him by phone after you'd briefed me." I'd used my jailhouse call to tell Paddy of the murder and to fill him in on the line I was taking with Dempsey. "Mr. Combs promised to back your statement about concerned friends — interfering friends from his point of view — calling us in. If pressed, he may be able to name a likely chum or two. One of them might even offer to give Combs an alibi for last night. He was a little vague on that point when we spoke.

"In addition to giving Dempsey Forrest Combs, I was obliged to make him a promise. The word on the street is that Kendall was only half owner of the Avalon. Dempsey would like to know the name of his silent partner. I told him we'd nose around."

"Why didn't he just ask Torrealba?"

"He did. The gentleman claimed ignorance. Lubos can do a punch drunk better than Max Rosenbloom, when it suits him."

"Speaking of Torrealba, how was it he happened by the club at three a.m.?"

Paddy was dousing his tamale with hot sauce. With the catsup disaster fresh in his mind, he waited until he was through to answer. "He'd just gotten home when Kendall's daughter phoned. Her name is Katherine, and I'm told she's all the family Ian Kendall had. Her father hadn't shown up, and she was worried. Torrealba was Kendall's right-hand man, so he was the logical guy to call. He'd last seen Kendall alive and well at the club. Kendall had offered to lock up, which was unusual, but not so unusual that Torrealba took notice. He drove back down to the club and found the front door, which I'm guessing you never even tried, unlocked. The rest you know all too well."

"Do you think Kendall met with someone?"

"We know he did, someone with a cosh. The question is, was he planning to meet with that someone?"

We sat down on a bench to eat our lunch. The bench was reserved in bold letters for the customers of the local trolley service, the Red Car. But, as Paddy observed, who hadn't been a customer of the Red Car at one time or another?

I said, "Suppose Kendall stayed late to talk with Baker. He must have talked to her sometime after we left, if he was the one who warned her off Combs."

"If he was. Torrealba couldn't remember when she left."

"What does she say?"

"I gather Dempsey is having trouble finding her. That may be another reason for his lack of interest in you. She hasn't left town by a train or plane. Ten to one, she hasn't left at all. We might have to have a look for her ourselves, if the police don't turn her up soon."

He wiped his hands, his mouth, and his tie with a paper napkin. "In the meantime, why don't we go pay our respects to Tip Fasano?"

"Fasano? You said last night he'd never have anything

to do with a movie."

"Movies, no. But murder. . . Eat up and we'll find out."

TWELVE

Tip Fasano could usually be found at a barbershop he owned on Figueroa. I'd always thought of it as a betting parlor with a striped pole out front, so I was surprised to find real barbers on duty and two of the establishment's three chairs occupied.

The gambler-owner was sitting in shirt sleeves in one of the bull-pen seats, reading a newspaper. The Ian Kendall murder was prominent on its front page.

Fasano and Paddy knew one another fairly well, though they weren't exactly lodge brothers. The gambler and I had more of a nodding acquaintance. We exchanged a couple now.

"First time I seen you in here, Maguire. Always figured your wife cut your hair at the kitchen table."

"So she does," Paddy said. "She books my bets in the dining room, so I won't be troubling you for that service, either. We can get right down to talking about poor Ian Kendall."

Fasano was almost as dark as Joel Jeffries, but nowhere near as clean cut. His nose looked like it had been batted around by Lubos Torrealba, and his eyes didn't open very far. They got extra narrow now as he worked at conveying puzzlement.

"Kendall? The bump-and-grind guy? I was just reading about him getting knocked off. Why come to me to talk about that?"

"You were one of his last visitors on this earth," Paddy said.

"Says who?" He looked at me, and the squint relaxed a bit. "So you were the hallway Romeo. I thought he looked familiar. Who was the broad? Tess Trueheart of the FBI?"

"Just one of Kendall's fillies," Paddy said before I could. I didn't want Fasano adding Ella to his list of troublesome witnesses.

Paddy continued, "You see, Mr. Elliott's getting hitched tomorrow."

Fasano saw, or thought he did. "Sowing some late entry wild oats last night, huh? Naughty, naughty." He returned his mail-slot gaze to Paddy. "So we both happened to be at the Avalon. Somebody tells the cops about me, maybe somebody else will mention Elliott here."

"They already know all about him. He found Kendall's body."

Fasano rustled his paper. "I don't read that in here."

"Check the late editions."

The gambler thought it out aloud. "The bulls had Elliott but they haven't been by to see me. So Elliott didn't mention me. This is what, a shakedown?"

"A conversation," Paddy said.

Fasano nodded to him but his eyes were back on me. Specifically, he was examining the top of my head, critically. I'd taken my hat off when I'd entered, gentleman that I was.

"You're getting married with your hair looking like that? You need a trim. Have a seat, we'll fix you up."

Paddy all but shoved me toward the open chair, his eyes twinkling like Victor Mature's teeth. I sat down, expecting one of the decoy barbers to step up—their customers having made themselves scarce—but Fasano sauntered over himself, shaking out one of the checkered cloths they used to drape the victims.

"Relax," he said as he fastened the thing around my neck. "I learned barbering in the army."

I'd had my share of GI haircuts, so I got less relaxed.

When he'd established a rhythm of combing and snipping, Fasano said to Paddy, "So converse."

My boss was seated now and lighting a cigar. "The police think Kendall had a silent partner at the Avalon, but they don't know who. We were thinking you might have been the man."

"So what if I was?"

"We believe that Kendall was planning to invest a lot of dough in a movie based on a Shakespeare play. Something the critics would love and nobody would pay to see. A guy who put his money in that would likely lose it, not that he'd care, seeing that he was doing the world a service. Still, the guy's business partner might object to the outlay, in a friendly way."

"He might at that," Fasano said.

I heard what sounded like someone stirring a coffee cup with a wooden spoon. Then Fasano was spreading lather around my ears. A minute later he was stropping a straight razor with enthusiasm.

"You do some first-rate figuring, Maguire. Too bad you stumbled out of the starting gate. Kendall wasn't my partner. He was my employee. I own the Avalon, right down to the last G-string. Kendall was strictly for show."

Another beard, I thought. Paddy said, "Why bother?"

I wished he'd held the question in for a minute. Fasano had begun scratching around my ears with the razor, and I wanted to let him concentrate.

"Our so-called reform mayor's already making things hot for the girlie shows. He won't be happy till he's driven them all out to Vegas and the gambling with them. If he knew a man in the gaming line owned the Avalon, he'd be that much friskier."

"So why risk the front you'd set up by going to the Avalon?"

I'd asked him that one. Then I felt more than saw him shrug.

"I've told you that much, so I might as well tell you the rest. I heard about Kendall maybe being involved in a movie deal and I dropped by to ask him about it. I happen to know his bank account is mostly air. He spent every nickel I paid him playing lord of the manor out in Granada Hills. I just wanted to be sure he wasn't writing any checks I'd have to cover."

"And?"

"He said he'd never even heard of the movies. Swore to it, as a matter of fact."

Paddy said, "Suppose he was holding back some money from the club, keeping two sets of books."

The gaming man laughed. "Not a chance. You think I'd let a guy with his reputation keep even one set of books?"

"Reputation?" Paddy asked innocently.

"Kendall got himself bounced from some wartime charity. That's how I was able to pick him up so cheap."

He spun me around so I was facing the mirror. "What do you think?"

I counted ears and said, "Looks great."

Fasano left me sitting there and went to write a note at the counter. "I'll give you the name of the adding machine jockey who keeps the tally for the Avalon. Go over and talk to him. Take your own accountant. Convince yourself that there was no dough leaking out of the club, that I had no reason to bother Kendall."

"That's awfully generous of you," Paddy said as he pocketed the slip of paper.

"The hell it is. I'm looking out for myself. The surer you are that I'm playing straight, the quieter you'll be. As it stands, I owe you big."

The man who never forgot an IOU, large or small, said, "Not at all."

Fasano freed me from the drop cloth and brushed at my shoulders with a whiskbroom. As I climbed out of the chair, I started to reach into my pocket from force of habit. I stopped, but not before Fasano noticed. His smile was almost natural.

"On the house," he said.

Luckily I had a question ready to fill the awkward silence. "What happens to the Avalon?"

"Torrealba can run it for as long as it stays open. Like I said, that business will end up out in the desert before we're ready to retire. In the meantime, it's not a bad little money maker."

"Even without Betty Ann Baker? The cops can't find her anywhere."

I'd slipped that in because I was anxious to see how Fasano would react. If Kendall had really been nothing more than a hood ornament, he couldn't have been Baker's sugar daddy. The gambler was a likely understudy.

"The farmer's daughter's gone back to the farm?" he asked with no interest whatsoever. "She'll take about a day to replace. This is Hollywood. The kind of grapefruit she was peddling grow bigger out here than anywhere in the world. Hell, the waitress who served me my hotcakes this morning could put Baker in the shade. In fact, I think I'll go by and offer her a career on the stage. That is, if we're done."

"Enjoy your lunch," Paddy said.

THIRTEEN

On the way to the Nash, we stopped to use a drugstore phone. I went first. Ella had already been brought up to date on my latest brush with the law by Peggy Maguire, but I wanted to check in. Unfortunately, she wasn't at her desk in the publicity department. I knew Paddy had more luck based on the amount of time he spent squeezed in the booth. He came out thoughtful.

"I just spoke to our friend on the force." He meant a certain guy who happened to be on Dempsey's payroll and Hollywood Security's both. "He tells me they haven't found Baker. I think we should tackle that next. Start by asking Combs. I'm told Dempsey interviewed him at home and left him there. If you hurry, he may still be in residence."

"And you?"

"I'm off to see Tip's accountant. It isn't every day that a

man in his profession offers you the run of his books. Maybe I'll find some nuts for a future winter."

Combs wasn't at home when I reached his aerie, but he got there before I left, tearing up in a prewar Bentley that deserved better treatment. For a minute, I thought he was going to handle me as roughly. Or try to. Then he remembered a previous engagement and brushed past me.

His important date was with his bar, a little wrought iron arrangement set up in the corner of his living room. I'd been socked on the jaw, kept up all night by the police, and shaved around the ears by a bookmaker turned flesh peddler, so a drink sounded good to me, too. Combs was a scotch drinker, like the late Mr. Kendall. He took it neat, which cleared the work space in a hurry. I stepped behind it and rummaged for Gibson makings.

"Help yourself," Combs said, using as heavy a hand with the sarcasm as he had with the hooch. "I'm in your debt after all. I understand it was you who arranged my visit from the police."

"That was my boss actually. You'd like him. He's as subtle as Wallace Beery except when it comes to the cops. Then he's Heifetz. Thanks to him, you got the royal treatment. If they'd hauled you downtown, tomorrow's papers would all have pictures of you holding your hands in front of your face."

"And what difference would that have made?" Combs asked wearily.

The weariness backed up my guess as to where he'd been since the cops left him. "Went to look for Baker?"

Combs's ice bucket was empty. I went in search of cubes

while he told me how he'd rushed to the Avalon and then to Baker's apartment without finding her.

"The police could have told you to skip those places," I said when I got back.

"They looked for her here." The memory made Combs alarmed and outraged in about equal parts. "Why on earth would they think Betty could be involved in a murder?"

By then I was done with my chemistry experiment. I carried my drink to a chair that faced Combs's sofa, settled in, and offered him a cigarette. He eyed my Lucky Strikes with mild distaste and offered me an alternative from a silver box. Dunhills. Despite that lapse in manners, I tried to console him.

"The cops want to talk with everyone who worked for Kendall."

The actor accepted that, grudgingly. To keep him with me, I said, "So you really did meet Baker in a library."

He nodded to his drink. "In Culver City, no less. Odd place to hear about Shakespeare. Odd to even bother with a lecture at my age, but I thought a little refresher course might be a good idea."

He gave me a searching look that took me by surprise. My first reaction was guilt. I'd been thinking just then that he needed to buy new cocktail onions and I was afraid he'd spotted my inattention. But no. Chewing that soggy onion had given me a skeptical air that Combs had misinterpreted.

"Why should I lie?" he asked. "So that lecture wasn't a refresher course. So it was my first exposure to a play I'd never even read. So what? What do my silly pretensions matter now?"

He was thoroughly embarrassed, and I was half a block

behind. "They didn't cover *The Tempest* at Oxford? Or was it Cambridge?"

"It was Wallops," Combs said with a croak that might have been a laugh. "Wallops School for Boys. In Manchester. I learned bookkeeping there, not Shakespeare. My father was a bricklayer and I was to be a clerk, which was as great a leap upward as any of us could imagine." He gazed out the window at his Grand-Canyon view. "Instead I somehow leapt all the way up here."

"Wallops must have had one hell of an elocution class."

"Actually, that was a private course of study. I taught myself to speak by listening to the radio and, later, the talking pictures. Ronald Colman was one of my instructors. All the old-timers were."

"Your heroes. And now, your fellow cast members."

"Exactly. I've always been self-conscious about my education. Dishonest about it, in fact. Ever since I landed this part in *The Tempest*, I've been terrified of being exposed. I've been studying hard so I could speak intelligently about the play.

"When I was told about the library lecture, I naturally made arrangements to go." He croaked his laugh again. "Incognito, of course. In my oldest clothes, a slouch hat, and windowpane spectacles.

"As soon as I stepped into the room where the talk was to be given, I spotted her, Betty Ann, though she was in disguise, too. A goddess made up as a housewife. She was as concerned about being recognized as I was."

By all those burlesque fans who hung around libraries. It was quite the fairy tale, with its prince disguised as a commoner meeting a princess disguised as a commoner and falling in love. A Hollywood fairy tale, in fact, which should have made it that much easier for me to swallow. And still it was going down harder than Combs's rubber onions.

"You said someone told you about this lecture. Who?"

"The producer fellow. Joel Jeffries."

FOURTEEN

When I'd descended to earth again, I found a phone in Chinese restaurant and gave Ella another try. She was back at her post and feeling nostalgic.

"Remember the first time we ate at Romanoff's?" The wistful question blindsided me. I'd been braced for something pointed on the subject of my night in the jug. "It was the day after we met. Remember that lunch, Scotty?"

"I remember losing an arm-wrestling match with a lady bookie. What brought that up?"

"I ate there today. That was part of my arrangement with a certain influential member of the fourth estate."

Suddenly the fried rice I'd order to backstop my tamale didn't seem so extravagant. "What was his name?"

"Hers, you mean. Natasha. She's one of Louella Parsons's legmen."

"Legwomen, you mean. She doesn't sound that influential."

"Take it from me, she is. If I'd said the wrong word, that *Tempest* movie would have been deader than its author. Brother, the tension was terrific. Thank God for whiskey sours."

I seconded the prayer, thinking the sours might explain Ella's lack of interest in my recent adventures. "So what did Natasha say about Combs?"

"I told her I was checking as a favor for a producer at Warners who was thinking of using Combs in a religious picture and wanted to be sure he was purer than Ivory Soap. Natasha said there hasn't been so much as a whisper about Combs since he landed. His social life is so quiet, Louella is convinced he's gay."

So much for her crystal ball. "Any chance Jeffries could have heard the news from someone else in the gossip business?"

"I don't think so. I think Mr. Jeffries was handing you a line."

"No hint about Baker?"

"Not in connection with Forrest Combs. She was mentioned in passing when we talked about Ian Kendall."

"Wait a minute. You talked about Combs *and* Kendall with this newshound? Wasn't that like keeping the matches in the same drawer with the gunpowder?"

"Scotty, everybody's talking about Ian Kendall today. That's the safest topic for small talk I could have come up with. And Natasha knew something interesting about him."

"That he liked scotch sours?"

"No, that he tried to interest Parsons and some of the other columnists in a story. It had to do with that old scandal Paddy mentioned. The one involving Aid for England."

"Kendall wanted to confess?"

"Just the opposite. He claimed to be the injured party. He wanted one of the papers to take up his case. Only none of them would bite. Who would take the side of a burlesque promoter against the British Colony?"

"What was Kendall's story?"

"Natasha couldn't remember exactly. It's been a year or more since Kendall tried to stir things up, and she didn't pay much attention then. Old news, she called it. Now she wishes she'd taken notes."

Her and me both. "Why is she suddenly interested?"

"Because Kendall's been murdered, silly."

"By the Hollywood Cricket Club? Sounds like Natasha's a little silly herself."

"It isn't that Natasha thinks Kendall's murder is connected to the old scandal, Scotty. It's just that Kendall's news now, so the scandal would be news today, even though it wasn't a year ago. The poor little guy. He could have gotten his story into the papers last year if he'd only known the secret."

"I'm guessing he'd have passed." My cardboard box of fried rice arrived. "I'll call you later about dinner."

"No more assignments, Chief?"

"You already have a job."

"Yours is more interesting."

If it was all right with the brothers Warner, it was all right with me. "Call the Culver City branch of the library and ask about a lecture on *The Tempest* they held recently. See if you can find out who sponsored it. And don't drive again for at least an hour."

"I shall not fail."

"Make that two hours."

FIFTEEN

I might have been given another assignment myself if I'd called into the office just then. So I didn't call. I went instead to visit Joel Jeffries Productions. Paddy had mentioned the address of the place during our drive out to the Santa Anita Racetrack, so I wouldn't think Jeffries was meeting us there because he lacked an office. The address was a very nice one on Hollywood Boulevard, not far from its famous intersection with Vine. The building I found there was a skyscraper by California standards, and Jeffries's suite was on its top floor.

I had all kinds of reasons to talk to Joel Jeffries. For one thing, I was as convinced as Ella that the producer had lied to us about being tipped to the Combs-Baker romance by a columnist. For another, Jeffries had sent Combs to the lecture where he'd met Baker, the very woman Jeffries had later sent us to buy off. That was quite a coincidence. My boss hated coincidences, but I saw them as opportunities, as little flags marking the locations of hidden connections. I thought there were all kinds of connections hidden in the current case and that Jeffries was just the man to unveil them.

Getting in to see the producer turned out to be a snap. The suite's reception desk was unmanned. In fact, there were indications that it had been cleaned out in a hurry. A couple of the drawers stood open and the blotter was cockeyed. I straightened it on my way to an open door through which was escaping a random tapping, like an amateur SOS.

Jeffries was seated behind one of those half-acre desks all producers had to have. He was back to me, facing a view that, while not the equal of Forrest Combs's, was still impressive, featuring as it did the distant skyline of downtown Los Angeles in all its hazy glory. The office's windows were wide open, and a hot breeze was blowing through the room. The tapping I'd heard was the work of an unsecured shade.

"Ahem," I said.

Jeffries swiveled around. He was in shirt sleeves, his tie undone. The wind had been running its fingers through his hair, maybe for hours. It had been an afternoon for drinking, but I didn't think Jeffries had joined the movement. For one thing, there was no sign of a glass or a bottle. Still, he had the look of a man who'd thrown the cork away.

One glimpse of his searching, bloodshot eyes, and I knew I'd been right all along. Ian Kendall had been the man behind *The Tempest*.

I didn't cozy up to it. "I wonder if anyone in the world took Ian Kendall's death as hard as you have."

Jeffries was gathering himself, but not to fence. "I suppose the man himself did," he said. "And there's his daughter. So you've figured it out, have you?"

"Not all of it. Maybe not half. But I know Kendall was your money man."

Jeffries's laugh was like a dry cough. Compared to it, Combs's croak was a regular babbling brook. "Money man? Promise man is more like it."

I looked around the windblown office. "He must have shelled out some."

"Not enough to pay next month's rent, never mind make a movie. I couldn't even pay my secretary what I owed her."

I sat down. "She took it in paper clips. Let's start at the beginning. Whose idea was *The Tempest*?"

"Kendall's. He contacted me, said he learned from a friend of a friend that I was interested in setting up as an independent. He said he had this dream about making a film of *The Tempest* and the money to back it up. Only he knew nothing about making movies and his name was mud in the best circles because of the business he was in. He thought we could help each other out. He gave me a list of his dream cast, with Ronald Colman at the top."

"And you knew Colman."

"Yes. I spoke with him right away. Colman was interested, but he was leaning toward a film of *King Lear*. That Oscar's really gone to his head. I ran that possibility by Ian, but he wouldn't hear of it. It was *The Tempest* or nothing. Luckily, Colman came around."

"Was Forrest Combs on that list?"

"Yes. Ian was as insistent on Combs as he was on Colman. I couldn't understand that. I wanted Richard Ney, as I told you and Maguire. But he wasn't available."

"If he had been, Kendall would have vetoed him," I said.

"But why?"

"I don't know yet. Let's move on to Combs and Baker. You didn't hear about them from any columnist, did you?"

"No," the producer admitted. "Ian told me. He convinced me we had to break it up or lose our stars."

"What reason did he give for not breaking it up himself?"

"He said Baker had some powerful friends."

"Did he mention any names? Tip Fasano, for instance?"

"No. He just said that he didn't dare cross her. He recommended I call Hollywood Security. That way he could stay out of it."

I paraphrased the question Paddy had asked at his kitchen table. "Why would Kendall let us anywhere near his club if he wanted to keep his tie to the picture a secret?"

"He was sure you'd never spot the link."

"On the subject of links, do you happen to know who got Combs and Baker together in the first place?"

"No," Jeffries said. He seemed to mean it, too.

"It was you. You told Combs about a lecture on *The Tempest* some library was hosting. And who should be waiting for him there but Baker."

I gave him plenty of time to mull that over. When he was done, he said something I didn't believe. "I read about that lecture in the paper. I thought Combs needed some additional grounding in the play. So I mentioned it to him."

After that, we finished the last of my cigarettes and the hot wind carried the smoke away. By and by, I noticed a wall decoration that seemed out of place: a framed photo of a warship. A baby flattop.

"Yours?" I asked.

"Yes. The *Gambier Bay*. Ever hear of her?"

"She was sunk off the Philippines, wasn't she?"

"Off Samar. The Japanese decoyed Halsey and his battle-ships away. Then they sent in the *Yamato* to mop up our inva-sion fleet. Largest battleship ever built. The only thing that stood in her way were some destroyers and escort carriers, like mine. Our pilots dropped everything they had trying to save us. They even dove on that monster with empty bomb racks just to buy us more time. But she got us in the end."

"How long were you in the water?"

"Not long. The Japanese admiral got cold feet and with-drew, just when everything was going his way. Of course, every minute you're swimming with sharks is one minute too many."

That was as much history lesson as Jeffries had patience for. "What am I going to do, Elliott? This will ruin me. I'll never work on another movie."

I'd wailed the same wail myself, which should have made me more sympathetic. I collected my hat. "Movie deals fall through every day. And independents fail. Nobody will make too much of this. Not unless the papers tumble to the Kendall angle."

"And what if they do?"

I broke my walk to the door to take one last look at the *Gambier Bay*. "Think of it this way. You've already gotten out of the worst jam you'll ever be in. You'll surely survive this.

"If that doesn't help, think of where Ian Kendall's spend-ing the afternoon."

SIXTEEN

I expected there to be a few cars in the Kendall drive. Friends from the country club who'd come by to console the daughter, Katherine, and maybe a police cruiser or two for color. But the drive was empty until I added the Nash. Which made it likely that the daughter was off somewhere listening to an undertaker's pitch. I'd have called before making the drive to Granada Hills, except that I wanted to see the house, wanted to verify that bit of Tip Fasano's story.

The gambler had said that Kendall spent all his dough playing lord of the manor. The house I found supported that. It wasn't exactly baronial, but it was nice, situated on a little rise with a front full of Versailles windows that were themselves full of the late afternoon sun.

I rang the bell, mostly as an excuse to get a closer look at the place. There weren't any weeds in the lawn, and the paint on the double front doors was a lot fresher than my shirt.

Before I could make up my mind to move on, the door was opened by a woman who probably heard "miss" and "young lady" a lot from salesclerks. That was because she was petite and thin to boot, with a child's wide eyes. A closer examination revealed her to be nearer the bitter end of her twenties than their rosy start. That today was especially bitter was conveyed by her black dress and a powderless sheen to her broad flat face that had to be the aftereffects of crying. It was Katherine Kendall herself, answering her own door on today of all days.

I had my hat in my hand by then and an apology on my lips for disturbing her. In the course of that, I mentioned my name and those wide hazel eyes came to life.

"You're the man who found my father."

Dempsey had been a little free with his information. But then, who was more entitled to know the facts than Katherine Kendall? Still, it was an awkward moment, easily the equal of my attempt to tip Tip Fasano. I braced myself for a shriek and a slammed door.

Instead, she said, "Won't you come in?"

We sat in a parlor so English it might have been a set from *Mrs. Miniver*. Tea was laid out on a low table. Only one of the dozen available cups had been used. She filled a second one for me and explained.

"I thought some people might be stopping by. We haven't many friends, but. . ."

I reached over and took the cup and saucer from her wavering hand. "The papers all mentioned your father running the Avalon. Your friends out here didn't know that?"

"Dad tried to be vague about it. Poor Dad. All his life he

was drawn to people who would naturally despise him. Like a dog who wants to be kicked."

Her accent wasn't English, but it was as close to it as an American girl was likely to get. I suspected she hadn't attended Wallops. I'd have asked her about it, but it wasn't my turn yet.

"Why have you come, Mr. Elliott? It wasn't to offer your condolences. You'd have shaved first."

She smiled a brave little smile when she said that, so I didn't go into my blushing routine.

"I'm trying to find Betty Ann Baker." It was what I was supposed to be doing, after all. If I accidentally stumbled across her in Granada Hills, so much the better.

"The police asked me about her," Katherine said musingly. "I had to admit that I've never even met her. Dad tried to shelter me from the Avalon. It was silly of him, really. I'm not a child and I knew where he worked. But Dad seemed to think if he didn't talk about the theater I wouldn't be tainted by it."

"But you knew to call Lubos Torrealba."

"Yes. I've often heard Dad speaking to him on the phone. Lubos was invaluable to him. He enabled my father to distance himself a little from the day-to-day running of the club. To pretend he was somewhere else, doing something altogether different."

"Like producing a motion picture?"

Katherine's interest in me caught its second wind. "You know about *The Tempest*? That was Dad's latest scheme, his last and greatest attempt to win the approval of people who never would approve of him."

"The British Colony?"

"Yes. The people who'd treated him so badly. To think of him selling his paintings and my mother's jewels just to impress the snobs who had wronged him."

"Over Aid for England?" I asked, surprising her a second time with my inside knowledge.

She set down her cup. "The police said you were in the Avalon this morning investigating Miss Baker. It sounds to me as though you've been investigating my father."

I couldn't see the harm in owning up to her. "I've been working for your father, though I didn't know it until this afternoon." I explained our original assignment and how Baker's remarks had made me curious about the man behind *The Tempest*. That gave me a segue back to the scandal.

"What actually happened at Aid for England?"

"Money disappeared," Katherine said. "But not into my father's pocket. The embezzler was a British major who'd been discharged from the army as medically unfit. A war hero. He'd come over from England to manage the permanent staff. The actors who lent their names to the charity made the tours and gave the speeches, but they weren't businessmen.

"A surprise audit revealed the shortage. Only two people could have taken the money, Dad and the major. He was above suspicion, a war hero and a member of the old boys' club."

"Your father had nothing to do with it?"

"No. The whole thing would have been hushed up, except that word of the shortage had leaked out. Someone had to be let go for appearances' sake. So Dad was sacrificed."

I said, "I only met him once, but he seemed like a member of the old boys' club himself."

"But then, you're an American. To the English, he stood

out a mile. His real name was Isaac Kendzurski. He was a Pole whose parents moved to England before the first war. His parents changed his name, but he would have done it himself as soon as he was able. He loved everything about England, including the awful weather."

"Then why did he come here?"

The brave smile flickered again. "Because he couldn't be an English gentleman in England. He could teach himself to speak like one and dress like one, but he could never really pass for one. Over here, among Americans, he could. He could be as English as Mountbatten.

"If only we'd settled in Cincinnati or Atlanta, everything would have been fine. But we had to end up here, in California, right next to the largest concentration of expatriate Englishmen in the country. Naturally my father tried to fit in with them and naturally they saw through him. And naturally they cast him out to protect one of their own."

Her eyes were wet, but she had herself well in hand. Her ersatz British father would have been proud.

"Then he told you he was going to back a movie starring those same actors."

"He didn't tell me, not willingly. I had to pry it from him after I noticed that the best painting in his collection was missing. I tried to talk him out of it. Tried to convince him not to waste what money we had on people who would never even thank him. He just laughed."

I sipped my tepid tea. Something about Ian Kendall's life story was oddly familiar. I realized that it echoed an autobiography someone else had shared with me earlier in the day.

I asked, "Did your father know an actor named Forrest

Combs?"

"Yes. They worked together at Aid for England. Father was closer to Forrest than any of the others. That may be why they sent Forrest to tell him he'd been sacked."

SEVENTEEN

I tried to phone in my report to Paddy, so I could get to Ella's as soon as possible. I was anxious to see if she'd made it home in one piece. But my boss wasn't taking a backseat to romance.

"Stop by and let's chat" was how he put it.

Paddy's office was made for early evening chatting, with its comfortable chairs, convenient smoking stands, discreet venetian blinds, and bottomless bottle.

The man pouring from that bottle went first. "The Avalon's books are so clean they'd let kids read them in Boston. Tip Fasano was telling us the truth. The Avalon wasn't financing the movie."

"But Kendall was," I said. "According to his daughter, he was selling off his paintings and her late mother's jewelry to do it."

That news flash stopped Paddy in the act of blowing the evening's first smoke ring. "You don't say. That should be easy to check, if he sold the stuff locally. In fact, I'm surprised I haven't heard about it already. Dumping enough art and ice on the local market to fund a movie should cause the kind of talk I make it a point to hear."

He suddenly came to attention without standing. "Hold it a minute. You spoke with Kendall's daughter? Tracking down Baker took you all the way out to Granada Hills?"

"In a manner of speaking."

He tapped the ash off his corona, settled in his chair, and went back to blowing smoke rings. "Start at the beginning," he said between rings two and three.

I did. I started with Combs and his desperate confessional mood, touching on Ella, who'd been in a great mood though somewhat confused. From there, I moved on to Jeffries, who'd been desperate, confessional, and confused. I ended up in Granada Hills with Katherine Kendall and her quiet dignity. Actually, I ended with her theory that her father had been bankrupting himself with a movie as a way of getting a pat on the head from the very people who'd previously kicked him in the teeth.

I kept my opinion of that idea out of my voice so Paddy could reach his own conclusion, which he did. "Did Kendall seem like that big a sap to you?"

"No. He was nobody's fool. Though he did work at being liked." I described the card trick he'd done for Ella.

"Sorry I missed that. I like a bit of sleight of hand."

Thinking back on that visit to Kendall's office reminded me of something I hadn't told Paddy. "While I was talking to Baker last night, Ella saw Kendall stick his head out his office door and bawl for Torrealba. The pug went into the office and came out a minute later carrying a box. I found that box on my return visit, just before I found Kendall. It had a bust of Shakespeare and copies of his plays inside. Kendall wanted that out of there so we wouldn't tumble to his interest in Shakespeare and spot the tie-in to the movie."

"Tumble to," Paddy repeated appreciatively. He loved it when I tried to talk like one of the boys. Then he shook his head. "You're working strictly on motivation again." It was his standard criticism of my technique. "You're forgetting little things like timing and cause and effect. When, for example, did you see Tip Fasano leave Kendall's little cubbyhole?"

"While we were waiting for Torrealba to announce me to Baker."

"Then you went in to see Baker, and Ella heard Kendall calling for his right-hand man. Then the box entered and exited."

"Right."

"So that box business had everything to do with Fasano and nothing to do with you. Kendall didn't even know who you were at that point."

"Jeffries could have told him."

"Fine. He knew your name, maybe even had a description. But he had no way of knowing you were there, not unless he had spies out on the runway.

"No. Kendall dumped his Shakespeare collection because Fasano said something on the order of, 'I heard about this *Tempest* movie. I don't want to hear about it again. Clean out this Shakespeare baggage or you'll be cleaning out the whole office.' End of dialogue."

"Fasano knows what a bust of Shakespeare looks like?"

"Who doesn't? Don't let's add snobbery to our other corporate failings. It's bad enough that Jeffries's retainer is all the dough we're going to see out of this."

He consulted his jumbo watch, which was lying in a nest of chain coiled on his desktop. "Time you were checking in with Ella. I'm sure you've things to talk about, tomorrow being the big day. But try to turn in early. You'll need your wits about you if you're going to find Betty Ann Baker before the cops do."

"Find Baker? The ceremony's at two. And Ella's sure to have things for me to do before then."

"Phone the list of errands in to Peggy. She'll have some of the other boys take care of them."

"Why can't the other boys look for Baker?"

"Because you're the only man I trust around that femme fatal, seeing as how you're safely blinded by love."

EIGHTEEN

We ate by candlelight in Ella's Salvador Dali dining room. We'd had reservations at a Greek place on Sunset, but the appointed time had come and gone during my sing-along with Paddy.

Ella wasn't quite herself during dinner. At first, I thought she was reacting to her fiancé showing up late with a bad haircut and a bruised jaw. Then I told myself she was just a little hung over. Finally, I decided she'd tell me about it when she was good and ready.

The problem wasn't that the *Tempest* business was overshadowing our impending nuptials. When I tried to steer the conversation to tomorrow's schedule of events, Ella yanked us back to the case with her report about the Culver City library.

"I couldn't get anybody at the branch to tell me who'd

paid for the lecture. They said the sponsor wanted to remain anonymous. But they did share the name of the UCLA professor who gave the talk. He sounded like a nice young guy on the phone. He was still trying to figure out why anyone would pay him a month's salary to deliver a class to five people and a dog. But he remembered who'd signed his check. Ian Kendall."

By then we'd taken our coffee into the parlor and settled on a sofa that looked something like a surfboard but wasn't as soft. Ella had a Stan Kenton disk spinning on her hi-fi. I was trying to convert her to Duke Ellington, but she was stubborn when it came to the arts.

"You knew all along, didn't you?" she said. "You knew it would turn out to be Kendall. How?"

Because every answer so far had been Ian Kendall. "Do you want to hear a crazy theory?"

"Yes," Ella said, but she sounded as though she'd rather have a tooth pulled.

I didn't have to start at the beginning. I'd recapped my report to Paddy as part of my excuse for being late.

"Joel Jeffries mentioned that Ronald Colman had countered the initial *Tempest* proposal with *King Lear*. Kendall said no."

Ella shrugged. "*The Tempest* is as good a play. And Prospero's a better role for Colman than Lear, even if he doesn't think so."

"Granted," I said. "But that isn't why Kendall balked. He wouldn't give up *The Tempest* because it would have screwed up his private symbolism. If I'm figuring right, *The Tempest* was the blueprint for his whole plan of revenge.

"In this plan, Colman's not Prospero. Kendall is. That

funny little guy who did card tricks is the deposed magician duke, stranded on a desert isle. Colman's one of the bad guys, one of the ones responsible for deposing the duke. Rathbone and all the other Brits are bad guys, too, because of what happened at Aid for England, because they tossed out Kendall to protect one of their own.

"Say it worked like this. Prospero, Kendall, was out for revenge. He had a sprite named Joel Jeffries gather up his victims for him, the same way Ariel brings all the heavies to the island in the play. Only Jeffries did it by producing a movie. He didn't know he was being used, but he was. And our Prospero had a beautiful daughter, played by Betty Ann Baker, who seduced the young prince, Forrest Combs.

"Combs was the key to the whole plan. The way I see it, Kendall never intended to make a movie. His real daughter, Katherine, told me he'd sold off paintings and jewels to fund the thing, but Paddy hasn't heard any scuttlebutt about sales that big. I think Kendall only sold enough to set up Jeffries in a nice office. Something that would dazzle the British Colony survivors.

"The next step was getting the intended victims' names linked to *The Tempest* in the trade papers. Then Kendall arranged for Combs to meet Baker by setting up a Shakespeare lecture and having Jeffries suggest to Combs that he go. Jeffries told me he'd seen an ad for the talk in the paper, but he was lying. He'd begun to glimpse Kendall's secret plan by then and he was scared.

"Next, Kendall got Jeffries to hire Hollywood Security to break up the love affair he'd arranged himself. He had Jeffries send me to the Avalon, where he was lying in wait. He had a bust of Shakespeare in his office and a copy of the play front and center in his bookcase. Just in case I showed up blind, he had Baker ready to tell me that Jeffries was a front."

Ella was keeping up so well she was actually ahead of me. "Only Tip Fasano came by and spoiled the big moment. He told Kendall that he'd heard about the *Tempest* deal. Kendall had to deny everything and rush the bust and the books out of his office before you could see them."

"That fits Fasano's story. But he might have been bending things a little, too. It works just as well if Kendall told him the truth about the *Tempest* scheme by way of proving to Fasano that no real money was changing hands. Fasano would still have pulled the plug. He wouldn't have wanted any bad publicity for the Avalon, and Kendall's plan was all about bad publicity."

Ella understood. "He intended for Hollywood Security to make the connection and leak the story. He wanted every paper in town to announce that the oh-so-proper British Colony was making a movie paid for by a strip joint. That would have hit those old actors where it hurt the most. In their reputations."

"Exactly where they'd hit Kendall during the war," I said. "They'd condemned him to a life of unrespectability, and he was going to give them a little taste of it. The British Colony would have been a collective laughing stock, with Ian Kendall laughing the loudest."

"Only he's not laughing, Scotty. He's dead. Who would crack his skull over a practical joke?"

Just then I was more interested in asking questions than answering them. I thought I finally understood what had dampened our evening. "You had this all figured out before

I showed up tonight, didn't you?"

Ella's nose was slightly crooked, the result of an old touch football injury. These days I only noticed it when I saw her in an unusual light or from an unusual angle. I noticed it now as she buried her face in my chest.

"I saw the broad outlines of it," she said. "After I'd found out that Kendall had set up that lecture and tried to keep it quiet. It made me sick to think that he'd thrown his life away for revenge.

"That isn't what *The Tempest* is about, Scotty. It isn't a play about revenge, not really. It's about rebirth, about Prospero coming back from the dead and getting a second chance. And he recognizes that. He knows he was a bad duke because he'd buried himself in his books on magic. He throws them all away at the end of his play. He wants to make good on his new life."

I realized that we weren't talking about Prospero by then or even about Ian Kendall. We were talking about Ella. When we'd first met, she'd told me about the men she'd known during the war and the wild life she'd led. A lot of that had happened after her brother had been killed overseas, and none of it mattered to me. I'd told her so more than once. Now, on the eve of our wedding, Ella's second chance and mine, the subject was back. For what I hoped would be its farewell appearance.

I raised her head with a finger under her chin. "I'm with Shakespeare," I said and got a kiss.

NINETEEN

The next morning, I set out early to find Betty Ann Baker. I also had a job or two to do for Ella, as I'd predicted to Paddy. She hadn't given me busywork, either, since her list included picking up both her flowers and her ring. I phoned those duties in to the office and hoped for the best.

For starters, I made the rounds of Baker's haunts. Then I interviewed as many of the girls from the Avalon as I could roust out of bed. None of them knew where Baker was or wanted her back very much. The competition was intense in the grapefruit business, as Tip Fasano might have phrased it.

I even put the Nash through one more climb up to Forrest Combs's. The actor wasn't at home, so I let myself in, certain that he wouldn't want me waiting around in the hot sun. I didn't find any blonde bombshells inside or any sign that one had stayed the night. In fact, if Combs had breakfasted there, the maid had been in since.

I had a seat outside on the bench with the bay view and went over my chat with Baker at the Avalon, trying to recall some throwaway line that might give me an idea where she'd gone. After I'd made a couple of passes and come up empty, I let the replay wander into the next scene, the one Ella and I had done with Ian Kendall. In Kendall's dialogue, I found what I'd been looking for. He'd said he'd discovered Baker when she'd been working in a bowling alley in Maywood. That snippet was all I had of Baker's past life. All I had to work with.

Unfortunately, Maywood was way on the other side of downtown Los Angeles. I was nearing the time when I'd have to break off and get dressed in my new suit, but I started out anyway, hoping the traffic lights would give a bridegroom a break.

Maywood's only bowling alley, the Victory Bowl-a-drome, was a stuccoed building with the curved roof of an aircraft hanger. It was already hot enough for the tar to be gleaming along the seams of that roof like parallel ebony rainbows. Inside it was cooler, if not quieter. Only a couple of bowlers were at it, but the clunk, trundle, and crash of their practice filled the place.

The proprietor was also the counterman that morning. His name was Muldoon, and he was built to juggle bowling balls. He was ex-navy, like Jeffries, judging by the tattoos on his forearms. I didn't ask if he'd been on the *Gambier Bay*. I'd had enough of secret connections.

I asked instead if he knew Baker. He demonstrated that he did by holding his hands up in front of his chest to form a massive brassier. He softened that by adding, "Nice kid, too. Never shorted the till. Course, with the tips she got, she didn't have to."

He went on to explain that Baker had worked as a cocktail waitress, though most of what she'd schlepped between the lounge and the lanes had been beer. She'd left without giving her two weeks' notice, and Muldoon hadn't even gotten a Christmas card since.

"I hope she's not in too much trouble with the law," he added. Baker's likeness had figured prominently in the newspaper spreads about Kendall's murder, mostly because she took a better photograph than her late employer. None of the stories had said more than that she was wanted for questioning.

"Nothing too serious," I said. "Did Betty Ann have any special friends around here?"

"Little Marie," Muldoon said. "One of the other waitresses. They were a real Mutt and Jeff team."

"Is Marie around?"

"Comes in at five, if she makes it tonight. She was scheduled for last night and never showed."

I liked the sound of that. I ended up paying Muldoon twenty bucks for Marie's address. On an average day I'd have gotten it for five, but this was no average, leisurely day.

The address was a short walk away, an apartment in an old house that had been subdivided to satisfy Southern California's endless housing shortage. Marie's establishment was the second-floor rear. I knocked on its door and listened. The only sound was a baby crying somewhere down the street.

The place was old, but the door was new and cheap. I

thought I could smell something through its many cracks. The smoke from a cigarette, but no ordinary one. I knocked again and heard the squeal of a window going up.

I stepped back and kicked the flimsy door in.

TWENTY

The noise of the splintering door created a little tableau in the room beyond. In the foreground, a chubby brunette had balled fists to her cheeks and her mouth open for a scream. Behind her, Forrest Combs was twisted at the waist to face me, an overnight bag in one hand. In the far distance, Baker, dressed in jeans and a gingham shirt, stood with one long leg out an open window.

The first to come out of the ether was Combs, who drew the little suitcase back like a football. I slid one hand into my suit coat, to where my gun would have rested if I'd been wearing it, and said, "Everybody relax."

Everybody did, even little Marie of the frozen scream. I sent her out to walk it off, and she scampered away willingly. Baker seemed almost as relieved as she slumped down onto an unmade daybed.

"Call the cops already," she said. "They can't be rougher than this hiding out."

I nudged a little smoking stand with my toe. In its amber glass tray, two Dunhill cigarettes were sending their expensive smoke curling up to the ceiling. "Call this roughing it? Nice job of fitting in, by the way. What did you send out for for breakfast? Partridge eggs?"

Combs had disarmed himself by then and joined his beloved on the rumpled sheets. I took one of the kitchenette's two chairs, planted it back toward them in the center of the room, and straddled it. "Let's hear it."

"I didn't kill Ian," Baker said. "Neither did Forrest. We were together when that happened, sitting on the beach near Castellamare. I was breaking things off with him."

"Seems it didn't take," I said.

Combs butted in. "Betty came to her senses this morning. She realized we were meant to be together and called me."

I thought it at least as likely that Baker had called him because she'd realized she needed serious carfare, but I didn't say so. Combs had enough bad news in store.

"If you've got an alibi," I said to Baker, "why are you hiding out?"

"Because I don't know why Ian was killed."

I finished the thought for her. "And you're afraid it might have had something to do with the scam you were helping him with."

It was Combs's cue to chime in with angry questions. What did I mean by scam? How dare I insult this flower of womanhood? He didn't chime.

Baker said, "He knows everything, Elliott. I told Forrest about Ian's plan to humiliate him and the others. And my part in it. He's forgiven me."

"She wasn't supposed to fall in love with me," Combs said, his voice all wonder. "That wasn't part of the scheme. But she did."

"When did she tell you her story?"

"This morning. As soon as I came to get her. She didn't want there to be any more lies between us. There won't be, ever again."

If ever a fish had swallowed the hook, it was Forrest Combs. "So there was never going to be a movie?"

"No," Baker said. "Just a little scandal. A tempest in a teapot, Ian called it. But he said it would be enough."

"Enough for what?"

"He never told me."

"Why did he call it off just before he was killed?"

"Tip Fasano threatened him. He'd heard about the movie deal somehow and stepped in at the last minute. We were so close, too. All we needed was for Hollywood Security to figure things out."

"Suppose we'd hushed it up." That being our standard fallback. "What then?"

"Ian planned to leak it to the papers himself, anonymously. Jeffries and everyone else would think you'd done it."

Paddy would love that. I shifted to Combs. "Was Kendall's version of the Aid for England business the truth?"

"I think so. I heard at the time that Ian was being sacrificed for the good of the work we were doing. But I never really knew the details. I was pretty much a glorified errand boy at the Aid offices."

"One of the errands they sent you on involved Kendall and an ax."

"Yes. They used me because I got on with Ian so well. We had a common bond, after all. We were both phony gentlemen. Breaking that news to him was the hardest thing I ever did. And the worst thing. I can understand his wanting to shame us. I certainly would never have hurt him over that. None of us would have. We'd all hurt him enough."

He put his arm around Baker, who was crying softly. "Give us a break, Elliott, can't you? We deserve a chance to make a life together. You of all people should understand."

"Me?"

The farmer's daughter tried to smile. "Yes. You're getting married yourself, aren't you?"

"How did you hear about that?" I was thinking of Tip Fasano, who'd been told about the wedding by Paddy, and wondering if Fasano and Baker might be pen pals after all. The answer turned out to be a lot simpler.

"Lubos told me. Lubos Torrealba. He said you'd mentioned it. He's in love himself right now and a sucker for other people's romances."

They were counting on me being the same kind of sucker. As it happened, I was.

"I won't call the cops," I said. "But my boss will want to talk to you. Stay put until he shows up."

The lovers were both teary by then. With their matching hair and china doll features, they actually looked like they belonged together.

"Thank you," Baker said. "And good luck."

I consulted my watch. "I'll need it."

TWENTY-ONE

Somehow I raced home without collecting a ticket, changed into a navy blue suit that made about as much sense on a steamy afternoon as woolen underwear, and got to the chapel before post time. But only just.

Luckily the Hollywood Security staff had come through for me. Ella's ring was ready and waiting. So were her flowers, as impressive a bouquet of gardenias as I'd ever seen. Peggy had assigned an operative named Lange to visit the flower shop. Less sensitive than your average fireplug, Lange was the last man I would have sent after posies, which shows what I knew about delegation.

"Lange didn't like the first bouquet," Peggy whispered to me on the chapel steps as she snagged my hat. "He leaned on the poor florist till the poor guy'd remade it, twice."

My best man, a screenwriter named Harold Meese, was

waiting by the side door that led directly onto the chapel's little altar. I'd shared an apartment with Meese and his cats before the war. As sweet a guy as he was, he hadn't been my first choice for best man. I'd given the nod to a service buddy named Merritt Jackson, who worked as a journalist in New York. But Jackson had been forced to leave his train in Kansas City, perhaps due to illness, perhaps because, as Paddy insisted, he'd spent the whole trip in the club car.

I was also doing without my parents' support. My mother wasn't feeling up to leaving Indiana, according to my father. I thought the real reason for their absence was my father's vow never to set foot in the Sodom that had stolen away his only son.

Ella's relations were likewise missing. In place of family, we had movie stars, a tradeoff many a bride and groom across America would have been happy to make. The biggest name in the small crowd present when Harold and I took our places was Torrance Beaumount, a professional tough guy who had shown up without a tie. Two rows in front of him was Gabrielle Nouveau, a.k.a. Annie Kovacs, a silent star who'd shared the screen with Valentino himself. Now she shared a mansion with a crowd of ghosts, Rudolph's among them maybe. I'd met her at Paramount when she'd been stubbornly sticking out a long-term contract despite the fact that she'd been offered her last script in 1937. It was tough to say who'd had more to drink, Beaumont or Nouveau. I only knew I was envying them both.

That thirst went away as the organist slipped out of the incidental stuff and into Ella's entrance music. First down the aisle was Ella's friend Maggie, who worked in the Warners typing pool. Then came the bride, escorted by Paddy, who had his chest stuck out like he was leading the St. Patrick's Day parade. Ella wore a pale blue suit with pill box hat and glowing eyes to match. She was wearing her sun- lightened hair up, which wasn't my favorite style. I consoled myself by picturing the moment when she'd yank the pins and let it tumble down. As if sharing that peep show, Ella smiled at me, crookedly.

When Paddy passed her off, I noticed that those smiling lips were trembling slightly. Her nervousness calmed me completely. In our informal rehearsals, I'd been the one who'd flubbed his lines. Now I rattled them off like the pro I'd once been and came through with a kiss at the end that was up there with Valentino's best work.

Or so said Gabrielle when she collared me at our reception. We held it at Mickey Lowlard's little restaurant on Western, a place so small that even our modest guest list had closed it to the general public. Even without the competition, seats were scarce, half the tables having been sacrificed to make room for a combo and a dance floor.

When Tory Beaumont claimed droit du seigneur in the form of a dance with Ella, I located Paddy in the bar. He had a pint glass in his hand and wouldn't listen to a word from me until I was similarly equipped. I wouldn't have bothered with a report just then, except that Ella and I were about to slip off to a lodge in redwood country and Ian Kendall's killer was still out walking around somewhere and Kendall had been our client, though once removed.

Still, I intended to make as simple a report as I could. I'd tell Paddy that I'd found Baker but not that she'd confirmed my crazy theory about Kendall never intending to make a movie, only trouble for some actors he hated. I'd mention

Kendall's real plan, of course, but I'd imply that Baker had sprung the idea on me, a bombshell from the bombshell.

I planned to play it modest for the same reason I'd tucked away my winning ticket back at Santa Anita. Paddy could be competitive at times. I didn't want a flare-up now, fueled by whatever the black beer was we were drinking. If he thought his legman was suddenly doing all the brainwork, Paddy might keep me in LA while he proved who really wore the larger hat.

As I expected, Paddy beamed like a proud parent through the part of the story in which I tracked Baker to Maywood. But the revelation of Kendall's revenge scheme didn't rock him back on his heels the way I thought it might. I wondered if he'd been thinking along those lines himself.

He was wondering about me, too. I'd overplayed my own stunned reaction to Baker's tale. He would have had the truth out of me in twenty questions or less, only Ella showed up.

"I hope you've been telling Scotty all about the birds and the bees," she said as she took my arm.

"He's been telling me, I think," Paddy replied. "But he wasn't quite through."

Ella was tugging me toward the door. "Expect the rest of it on a postcard," she said.

TWENTY-TWO

Someone had actually tied tin cans to the rear bumper of the Nash. It was a practice perpetuated—if not invented—by the movies, so I should have expected it to happen in Hollywood. Ella insisted on driving a block with them in place. Then she took pity on me.

An hour after she'd snatched me from Paddy, we had the car undecorated and packed and were pulling away from the curb in front of her apartment. I think she sighed, but I had the top down and the wind noise made it hard to tell. She definitely sidled up next to me and put her arm under mine.

Then she said, "Ian Kendall would have enjoyed this."

"Right about now he'd enjoy going to the proctologist," I said to cover my guilty start. I wondered how Ella had known I was thinking about Kendall, the unfinished business

I was leaving behind.

"I meant," Ella said, "that he would have seen our wedding as fitting right into his scheme. He planned for everything to parallel *The Tempest*, right?"

"Right."

"Well, our wedding is kind of like the masque. You remember me telling you about that, don't you? It's that little play Prospero conjures up for the two lovers, Ferdinand and Miranda, a kind of pageant on love and fertility that interrupts the main story right at the end."

"Like a musical number in a Marx Brothers movie," I said. "I remember. But our wedding didn't interrupt Kendall's scheme. That ended when he died."

"His plan ended, but not his story. We still don't know who killed him or why. So our wedding fits right in. Kendall would have loved that."

"It only fits if we're a scene away from solving the thing."

Ella gave my shifting arm a tug. "I was kind of hoping you were, Scotty. So you'd be free to focus on the honeymoon. I'd hate to have you drifting off during sex. Not for the first ten years or so."

I started to ask her if she thought I was that big a dope, but I didn't want to know the answer. Not for the first ten years or so.

I said, "If everything fits so well with *The Tempest*, maybe we should be looking for the killer in the play. Too bad nobody murders Prospero."

"Caliban tries to," Ella reminded me, "but he doesn't pull it off."

"We don't have a Caliban." I was thinking back on how

I'd cast the play for her the prior evening, with Kendall as Prospero, Combs and Baker as Ferdinand and Miranda, and Joel Jeffries as Ariel, the sprite who makes things click. It occurred to me that I'd been wrong about that part. Kendall's sprite and confidant had really been Betty Ann Baker, her magic power being her body. Recasting Ariel left the Miranda part vacant. Luckily, Kendall had a real daughter, Katherine, to fill the void.

That chain of thought explained how I happened to be thinking of Katherine Kendall when Ella said, "There's Lubos Torrealba. For Caliban. He was Kendall's lift-and-carry guy, after all."

I slowed the Nash, dropping out of traffic and grinding my whitewalls against a curb. "Wasn't Caliban in love with Prospero's daughter?"

"You think Torrealba is in love with Baker?" Ella asked. And then, exasperated, "Is there any man who's not?"

"I was wrong about Baker being Miranda. She told me today that Torrealba is goofy for some woman, but she didn't say who. Suppose it's Kendall's real daughter, Katherine. She and Torrealba could have met in a dozen different ways."

"Suppose they did. What does that get you?"

Another hidden connection, possibly *the* hidden connection. "Katherine told me she'd tried to talk her father out of selling everything they had to finance a movie. He just laughed at her."

"Of course he laughed," Ella said. "He knew there was never going to be a movie."

"But she didn't. He never let her in on anything that might sully her, including the truth about his *Tempest* scheme. For all she knew, her father really intended to produce them into the poor house. And then there's Lubos Torrealba. If she'd fallen for him, her father would have been a major obstacle. Torrealba was the last guy Kendall would have wanted to be introducing around the country club as his son-in-law."

"Oh, Scotty. His own daughter. Do you really think she could have been involved?"

"What do you say we ask."

TWENTY-THREE

Granada Hills was on our way to the honeymoon lodge, which is to say, it was slightly north of Ella's place. We got there just after dark. My original plan had been to confront Katherine Kendall directly, to shake her up. But the more I thought back on our tea party, the less Kendall seemed like someone who'd shake easily. So I settled for parking the Nash a little way from the house and putting its roof up.

Lights were burning in the Versailles windows. "Looks like she's expecting someone," I observed.

"I hope he hurries," Ella said. "I had a lot of champagne at the reception. Nice house. Nice neighborhood. To think of Kendall risking all this for revenge."

This time I was sure she'd sighed. She slumped away from me, too, rehashing, I was also sure, the complaint that had gotten her so down the prior evening, namely that Kendall had missed the true meaning of *The Tempest* by going after revenge instead of rebirth. I tried to think of some way of exonerating the little guy and saving Ella's mood. Against heavy odds, I did.

"I was wrong about Ian Kendall," I said. "He wasn't after revenge. He wanted a second chance."

"Scotty, he was slipping a whoopee cushion under a pack of stiff-necked actors. How is that getting a second chance?"

"Remember what Louella Parsons's assistant Natasha told you? She said Kendall tried to get the papers to take up the Aid for England story last year and nobody would."

"Right," Ella said. "It was old news."

"But Natasha also said that they'd run the story today if they had it. Kendall's murder made it newsworthy when it hadn't been last year. And you joked that Kendall could have gotten his little exposé in print if he'd only known the secret, which was to tie it on the tail of some contemporary story, like his murder."

"I remember," Ella said, sounding hopeful.

"I think Kendall knew the secret, knew what he had to do to get the papers interested in the old story. He dreamed this whole *Tempest* deal up to create a contemporary scandal the papers would love, and one that would tie directly to the story he really wanted them to run, the Aid for England frame-up. Baker told me Kendall had said the *Tempest* fracas would be just big enough. He meant it would be big enough to hook the tabloids."

My wife's eyes were damp. "I can see him smiling at the reporters when they came to interview him. And maybe doing card tricks for them. He would have had his reputation back, his second chance. Scotty, he did understand the play. Thank you."

She topped that with a kiss. We were still at it when a car crept past us and pulled into the Kendall drive.

"Show time," I said and opened my door.

"Be careful. Remember what he did to you the last time."

I told her to head for the nearest house and call the cops. Then I set off at a run, across the street and up the slopping lawn, anxious to get to the front door before the driver of the creeping car could slip inside. Luckily, the sedan had barely crawled its way to the top of the drive.

A man got out as I dropped to a stroll. A hulking man. Caliban in the flesh.

"Evening, Lubos," I said.

He didn't reach for any hardware as he whirled around, so I didn't dive for the azaleas. "You must really have it bad to show up here before your boss is safely in the ground. What did you use on him, by the way, a hunk of pipe?"

He preferred demonstrating to answering, coming for me in a fighter's crouch. But he hadn't caught me stooping over a corpse this time. I'd boxed a little myself in the service. And I'd seen Torrealba in the ring. I parried his left jab with an open palm and stepped inside his roundhouse right just as my own left popped his eyes open. Then I sat him on the grass with a right that had no loop in it whatsoever.

My moment of triumph was stepped on by a voice from the front steps that called me the name Combs had used earlier. "Bastard!"

I turned and saw Katherine Kendall in a negligee right off the rack at the Avalon. She held a glittering automatic, pointed at me.

"If you've hurt Lubos—"

Her threat was cut short by a big guy who moved like a dancer. Paddy Maguire. Before she could react, he was behind her, squeezing the blood out of her wrist.

Just as he secured the gun, Ella trotted up, a high heel in each hand. "The police are on the way. Point me at a powder room."

TWENTY-FOUR

Paddy tried to hustle us away before the cops arrived, but Ella's little emergency gave me time to quiz him.

"How did you get here? Were you following us?"

"You two? No. What kind of Peeping Tom do you think I am?" He'd had an unlit cigar in his teeth when he'd stepped up to waltz with Kendall. Now that she was safely tucked away in the backseat of Torrealba's sedan, he took a moment to light it. "I was following your sparring partner."

"Torrealba? You figured out he was Caliban?"

"Caliwho? What in blazes— On second thought, don't tell me. I prefer to think Ella married a full crate of eggs."

That made two of us. "So why were you following Torrealba?"

"After you headed out, I had a nice chat with Betty Ann Baker. She told me all, including how she and the late Mr.

Kendall would have been home free if someone hadn't spilled the beans to Fasano. That started me thinking about who the blabbermouth might have been. It had to have been someone who thought the movie deal was kosher, since that's the story Tip came to see Kendall about. I should have asked Tip the name of his source yesterday in the barbershop, but I was distracted by the sight of you squirming in his chair. Anyway, I called him tonight and rectified the omission."

"And he told you the source was Lubos Torrealba."

The man in question was trying to rise from his seat on the grass. Paddy tapped him on the side of the head with a lump of lead wrapped in leather, and he settled down again. Then, swinging the sap like a nightstick, Paddy continued the lecture.

"That begged the question, who had told Torrealba? Kendall could have himself, of course, but then Torrealba probably would have known that the movie was a fraud. Of all the people who thought the movie deal was legit, only one knew Torrealba, the woman who supposedly called him the night her father didn't come home from work. I was betting Lubos would lead me to her, and he did."

A more relaxed Ella had rejoined us by then. Paddy kissed her on the cheek. "Forgot to do that back at the restaurant. Now move along, you two. I'll explain things to Dempsey and his friends in words of one syllable. And I won't mention cannibals or fairies."

"What about Ian Kendall?" Ella asked.

"What about him? They'll bury him, if they haven't already."

"That's what I mean, Paddy. What about his funeral? Who's going to be there? His only relative will be in jail."

Ella had had a lot of champagne. She'd have volunteered me as eulogist, if Paddy hadn't stepped in.

"Leave everything to me. I'll see things are done right. Now skedaddle."

We broke our drive north at the romantic town of Fresno and got to the lodge the next day in time for lunch, though we skipped the actual meal. Two days later we did make it down to the dining room for breakfast. Ella had collected an LA paper at the front desk. She was deep into it as soon as we sat down.

"Now I know we're married," I said.

"Shut up and listen to this story. 'British Colony buries one of its own. Yesterday the cream of Hollywood's English contingent turned out to bury slain theatrical producer Ian Kendall, fifty-two. Kendall's pallbearers included actors Ian Hunter, Allan Mowbry, Reginald Gardiner, and Forrest Combs. Sir Cedric Hardwicke read the Rupert Brooke poem containing the line, "If I should die, think only this of me, that there's some corner of a foreign field that is forever England." ' "

Ella paused to sniff before reading on. " 'Ronald Colman recited lines from Shakespeare, "We are such stuff that dreams are made on, and our little life is rounded with a sleep." ' Scotty, that's from a speech by Prospero! How did Paddy do it?"

"Blackmail. He must have convinced them he knew all the dope on the old Aid for England business."

I was moved to quote Prospero myself. " 'Our revels are now ended,' I guess."

Ella could beat me at that game all day. " 'Hush and be

117

mute, or else our spell is marred,'" she said, rising and taking my hand. "And I do mean you, bub."